Sharp Horns
on the Moon

Sharp Horns
on the Moon

CAROLE CROWE

~2000~

To Megan,
Enjoy!
Warmest wishes from
the Virgin Islands
Carole Crowe

BOYDS MILLS PRESS

I wish to acknowledge the Soares of Anegada: the children, who went to school in a small boat; the father, who fished far from home; the mother, who watched from shore, a beacon for their safe return.

Thank you to Larry Rosler, my editor, for opening the door, and for his kindness and patience and wisdom.

And my loving gratitude to Jack, who reads every word I write, over and over.

Text copyright © 1998 by Carole Crowe

Published by Caroline House
Boyds Mills Press, Inc.
A Highlights Company
815 Church Street
Honesdale, Pennsylvania 18431
Printed in the United States of America

Publisher Cataloging-in-Publication Data
Crowe, Carole.
 Sharp horns on the moon / by Carole Crowe.—1st ed.
[144]p. : ill. ; cm.
Summary : A girl, who lives on an isolated section of an island, befriends the ghost of a girl who died mysteriously years before.
ISBN 1-56397-671-4
1. Ghosts—Fiction—Juvenile literature. [1. Ghosts—Fiction.]
I. Title.
813.54 [F]—dc20 1998 AC CIP
Library of Congress Catalog Card Number 97-72771

First edition, 1998
Book designed by Tim Gillner
The text of this book is set in 12-point New Baskerville.

10 9 8 7 6 5 4 3 2 1

In memory of Pam, my angel, my friend,

and for Tara, my daughter, with love

Sharp Horns . . .

I KNOW MY MOTHER WAS BESIDE ME *that afternoon in front of the jasmine house, when Daddy and I were house-hunting in town for the last time. Jasmine. The bushes grew wild along the fence, the scent of the tiny white flowers so sweet the air felt sticky. I know my mother tried to guide me past the house with an urgency I didn't understand. Yet I resisted her, as I would resist years later. Or perhaps the house held a power of its own.*

Like a man's cap with a jaunty tilt, the red slate roof hung low over sparkling windows that seemed to stare at me in surprise. The cherry-red door like a mouth saying "Oh!" made me laugh and clap my hands. "Daddy, Daddy," I cried. "Wait! Let's look at this house." But Daddy kept walking, his shoulders hunched around his ears, like a turtle pulling into its shell.

Then darkness fell in an instant and a crescent moon with devil horns sliced through a night sky. The house filled with a haunting glow that drew me through the creaking gate, to the red door that eased open on its own.

It was my father who broke the spell. He yanked me from the doorway and night turned back to day. It would be many years before I returned to that house, not knowing what danger might await—and not caring.

. . . on the Moon

ONE

I floated facedown above Boneyard Reef. Strands of my long brown hair swirled around my head and in front of my face like the arms of a giant octopus. I took a deep breath through my snorkel. It sounded strange and hollow. A cloud swallowed the sun and cool air spilled over my back. As I floated, I watched a dark shape ease out of the waving grass below, strike at a small passing fish, then disappear into a crevice of coral with its catch.

The ocean began to pulse softly. I hung in the silence and let it throb through my body like a beating heart. I knew what it was and waited. The throbbing grew stronger and stronger until finally I heard the engine of the approaching boat. I kept my head low as the mail boat eased up to our small dock. I didn't want the captain telling my aunt I was swimming the reef alone again.

My stomach knotted when he jumped to the dock with the parcel of home-schooling books for my first year of high school. I thought of my father's broken promises and yanked the mask down roughly over my face. It fogged immediately and I ripped it off, wrapped the rubber strap around my wrist, and dove.

With my eyes squeezed shut, I pictured my father somewhere on the ocean fishing. He'd been saying his fishing trips had gotten longer because he was trying to save enough money for a house in town so I could go to school with other kids when I started high school. I knew it wouldn't happen, but that hadn't kept me from hoping.

I blew out the last of my air, and on the way up, I pictured a huge school of fish changing direction, swimming toward Mystic Island. In my mind, my father altered course and followed the school in his fishing boat, a school that led him home to keep his promise.

I sucked in a deep breath of air and dove again toward the forest of coral on a shallow ledge. I'd been swimming the reef alone since I was eight or nine, pretending I was a deep-sea diver discovering sunken treasure in one of the broken ships at the bottom of the reef.

Then I closed my eyes and let the loneliness weigh me to the bottom, the worst loneliness I'd ever felt. Would I always live in the only house at the far end of Mystic Island? Would I never go to a real school or have a friend?

Suddenly a light burst in front of me, so brilliant it shone through my closed lids. My eyes flew open. The light pressed into my face. I slapped my hands against it and tried to turn away. But it circled and closed in again. In the center of the light, I saw the shimmering image of a girl's face. She stared into my eyes with an intensity that terrified me. I tried to surface, but the force of her radiating light seemed to hold me under. Then, as quickly as she'd come, her face disappeared, and a shiny gold coin flickered in the light and spun to the sandy bottom.

I clawed my way to the surface, crying and choking,

and drank in the sweet air. I hugged my arms tightly and wondered if this was really happening or if it was one of those dreams I sometimes had that seemed so real after I woke up.

I stared below at the gold coin in the sand and waited for the shiny sparkle to fade just like that girl's face had disappeared. But the coin continued to glow. That's when I felt a warm touch on my hand—a touch I hadn't felt in years. When I was a little girl, lonely or frightened, I'd believed it was my mother come to hold my hand and make everything all right. I was so young when she died that I couldn't remember a thing about her, but she must have loved me very much because she would always find her way back to me whenever I needed her. It was only when I got older that I felt her near me less and less, until finally I wondered whether she had ever been there at all.

An easy wave lifted me and the pressure on my hand seemed to turn me away from the coin. *Could it be my mother?* I wondered. I slapped my palm against the water. *Of course not.* It was just my imagination—that's what my Aunt Ethel would say—and I started to dive. But something *was* holding my hand. It tugged at my arm to keep me from diving. I shivered and stared at the gold spot just below me.

Ignoring the feeling, I kicked down to the reef and snatched at the bright spot in the sand. I squeezed it tightly in the palm of my hand and was about to surface, my breath running out, when a light slid from between the cracked ribs of a Spanish galleon and floated up slowly toward the ledge.

A cloud must have curled around the sun then and

cast shadows below, because the strangest thing happened. The light shimmered and again the face appeared, but it looked bloated and ugly like the face on a drowned body. Then it turned into the face of that same girl, a girl my own age. My chest burned from lack of air, but I couldn't pull my eyes away as the girl opened her mouth and swallowed a fat silver fish. She grinned and began to move toward me.

I crashed through the surface, gasping for breath, and began kicking and swimming wildly toward shore. I didn't know what might happen if she held me under again. I dragged myself onto the sand and fell to my knees. I stared at my clenched fist, almost afraid to open it, breathing so hard I was getting light-headed. I uncurled my fingers slowly and looked down at the palm of my hand, and there it was—a Spanish coin from a ship that had sunk hundreds of years before, a gold coin so shiny it looked like it had been minted that very day. I heard a sound and jumped up to look behind me, almost expecting to see the girl with a fish hanging out of her mouth. But as always, I was alone.

A sudden breeze blew stinging sand across my legs and rustled the trees. Jasmine filled the air, jasmine so real, so sweet, I could have been standing in front of that house from long ago. I looked around to be sure of what I already knew—there wasn't a jasmine bush in sight. I closed my fingers over the warm gold coin and stared out toward Boneyard Reef.

As usual, Aunt Ethel, Dad's older sister, was in the middle of a big conversation with herself when I raced into the yard. She dragged a dry sheet from the line strung between two palms and dropped clothespins into the large pocket of her apron.

"Miracle that rain didn't come down before now. I'll end up rinsing these sheets all over again and drying them tomorrow."

I looked up at the blue sky, searching for that one little rain cloud Aunt Ethel would track down like a hawk. A breeze blew gray hair in front of her eyes and a pillowcase fell to the ground when she brushed at her face.

"Oh, for pity's sake!" She snatched the case up, shook away some imaginary dirt and glared up at that rain cloud in the distance. Aunt Ethel didn't like being deprived of her misery. She could *will* that rain cloud over our yard. I knew that deep down she'd be "pleased as punch" when she discovered that the clean sheet in her arms was trailing in the dirt. I tiptoed toward the back of the house.

"Ivy Marie Bell! You stop right there. Now where have you been all afternoon? Grab the rest of those clothes before it rains."

"I don't think it's going to rain, Aunt Ethel." I pushed the coin deep in my pocket.

"You haven't been out by that reef, have you?"

"I was hanging out at the beach," I said, trying not to tell the truth without exactly telling a lie. My aunt went kind of crazy the first time she found me snorkeling the reef. When Dad came home from his fishing trip, she carried on forever, telling my father to forbid me to snorkel alone.

"More man-eating sharks in that water than mosquitoes in August!" she yelled. "And she could get a cramp. That'd be the end of her, you can bet your bottom dollar on that!"

5

"But, Dad," I'd pleaded, "they're only nurse sharks. They won't bother me."

"Ivy—," Dad had said, and I just knew he was going to tell me not to do it again.

"Dad, I like the fish. They're my friends. And Mom would never let anything happen to me. Never."

Dad's rough, tanned face saddened a little. I knew he still loved my mother, even though she'd been dead for so many years. Sometimes I wondered if the long fishing trips were his way of escaping the memory of her. We didn't even have any pictures of my mother. Aunt Ethel said he got rid of them after she died.

"Albert, don't you encourage this ghost business with her mother. She's dead and buried, God rest her soul." Aunt Ethel always got jittery when I talked like my mother was still around.

Finally, my father said very seriously, "Don't upset your aunt," and we just sort of stared at each other.

Aunt Ethel marched away mumbling, "Fish friends, indeed," triumphant over saving me from myself.

My father tucked my hair behind my ear with one of his calloused fingers. "The sea deserves respect, Ivy. Stay alert."

I decided right then and there that he was giving me permission to snorkel, but telling me to be careful and to keep it from my aunt so she wouldn't be upset.

Still, I never felt good about deceiving her, even when she drove me crazy, which was most of the time. Sometimes I wondered if I were really fooling her at all. She never pressed me about where I went every afternoon or came looking for me like she used to do when I was younger. I think she might have felt a little sorry for me because my mother was dead and my father was away so often. I guess she felt sorry, too, that I didn't have any friends. We were far off the Florida coast, and our end of Mystic Island was still undeveloped. There were no roads cut through the thick scrub, and ours was the only house so far from the other end of the island, fifteen miles from the school and other kids. We were so remote, even the telephone lines didn't come out to where we lived.

We'd just finished taking all the clothes down—except for my only good dress, the one with the tiny blue flowers, still damp around the collar—when the first raindrop plopped on my aunt's nose. Her face perked up as she waited for it to pour, expecting the laundry and us to get soaked. But the cloud passed by without another drop, and Aunt Ethel glared at it like it had personally ruined her afternoon by not dumping buckets on us. When she spotted the sheet trailing in the dirt, she snapped her head at me once, like she'd just been proven right, and marched into the house.

I hooked the lock on the inside of my bedroom door, so my aunt wouldn't surprise me, and fished the coin out. I rubbed my thumb along the smooth edges and bounced it in my palm, thinking about that girl I thought I'd seen.

Don't be stupid, Ivy, I said to myself. *It was just a dumb cloud making shadows.*

That's when I heard a laugh outside my window, a girl's laugh as clear as a glass bell. I couldn't imagine who would be out there, since ours was the only house at this end of the island. I stuck my head out and looked around.

A pebble hit the window by my face and I clunked my

head when I looked to the left. Standing near the clothes-line, wearing my very best dress, was the girl who had swallowed the fish.

Very slowly, I squeezed my eyes shut. Then opened them again, expecting her to be gone. But she still stood there, arms folded, watching me intently.

"That's my dress," I called out, rubbing my head where I'd hit it.

She just stared at me. Then she reached in the front pocket and pulled out a fish, which flapped at the end of her fingers. "I need a place to keep this," she answered.

I just about broke my leg climbing out of that window. "Get that smelly fish out of my pocket! You'll stink up my dress."

"Ivy Marie! Who are you talking to out there?" Aunt Ethel charged out the back door. The girl grinned and dropped the fish back into the pocket of my dress. She folded her arms and tapped her foot on the dirt, waiting to see what I'd do next.

"Who's got a fish in what pocket?" Aunt Ethel looked over her shoulder and stared at the very spot the girl stood, but she obviously didn't see a thing.

"Who were you talking to?"

If there was one thing I didn't want to do, it was get my aunt all worked up about ghosts. She had some superstitions about them that I didn't understand.

The girl took the fish out again and gave it a little wiggle. Aunt Ethel was getting jittery like she used to when I was little, before I'd learned not to mention my mother coming back to hold my hand.

"I guess I was just talking to myself." I narrowed my

eyes at the girl who was still grinning at me. "Aunt Ethel, don't you think we should take my dress in? Just in case it starts to rain?" *Let's see what you do about that, fish girl.*

My aunt stepped in front of me, her hands on her broad hips. "Sometimes I don't know what gets into you," she said. She pressed her hand on my forehead like maybe I was burning up with fever. When she turned and walked to the clothesline, the girl had disappeared, and my dress was pinned up like she had never even worn it.

Aunt Ethel yanked it down and handed it to me. "Come in and get washed up, Ivy. And the potatoes need scrubbing." She turned back once and caught me sniffing the pocket of my dress.

"*Whatever* has gotten into you today? That's the trouble," she said, bustling away. "Alone too much. Well, it's a good thing your father's due back the end of next week."

My dress didn't smell like an old fish when I pressed it tightly to my face. It smelled like a rainy night.

"*What's your name?*" I whispered.

She didn't answer. But I knew she was there, right beside me.

TWO

The next morning when the sun came up, I climbed out my bedroom window and waited for her in the yard. I even hung my dress on the line and sat perfectly still on the cool ground. I waited over an hour, but she never came.

I figured the reef would be the next place to check. Maybe she needed to eat fish or something. I had a lot to learn about ghost friends.

I climbed back into my bedroom and dressed quickly, then crept toward the kitchen to grab a piece of fruit before Aunt Ethel woke up and made me eat a big breakfast. But she must have gotten up before dawn.

Aunt Ethel was beside herself, all alone at the kitchen table, talking to nobody, turning pages, and slamming down one textbook after another.

"How's a person supposed to understand any of this gibberish? X equals this and Y equals that. Nothing equals anything, for pity's sake." She flipped the pages of my new math book, shaking her head. She pulled her glasses off repeatedly and rubbed them clean on her cotton dress, as if seeing better would make everything clear.

I got a little beside myself, too, thinking about another year of studying with Aunt Ethel. There was nothing in the world I wanted more than to go to a regular school and have friends—maybe a best friend who would meet me at my house and walk with me, our arms linked together. But the new term was starting in a month or so, and I still hadn't talked my father into looking for a house in town. I'd still be home-schooling my first year of high school, teaching Aunt Ethel algebra, pretending she was the one teaching me.

Very slowly, I tiptoed backward, so my aunt wouldn't see me, but a creaky floorboard in the hall gave me away.

"Ivy? Is that you? Come and look at your books. You'll have to keep your nose to the grindstone this year, young lady."

I dragged myself back into the kitchen, rubbing my nose. When I was little and first started home-schooling with my aunt, I used to wake up every morning and feel for my nose, to make sure a grindstone—whatever *that* was—hadn't worn it flat in the night.

Aunt Ethel stacked my books and sighed loudly. "No monkey business this year, I can tell you that. You can't be disappearing for hours at a time once you're doing high school work. It's serious business this year, mark my words."

"Good morning, Aunt Ethel." She looked so worried that I almost smiled. She got the same worried look every year when my new schoolbooks arrived. I couldn't help but give her a little peck on the cheek.

"I'm not hungry," I said as she turned the gas jet on and slapped a spoon of butter in the skillet. "Aunt Ethel, *really*, I'm not hungry!" I sighed just as loudly as she did, but she poured that pancake batter into the hot skillet like she hadn't even heard me.

"Wouldn't that be lovely?" she said to herself. "Her father comes home and finds I've let his daughter starve to death."

I watched the empty yard from the kitchen window, listening for the girl's musical laughter, but all I heard was my aunt's constant chatter. When she called me back to the table, I groaned at the tall stack of pancakes on my plate.

Aunt Ethel opened her eyes wide as I started to eat. "Well, for pity's sake. One minute she's not hungry and the next she's eating like I haven't fed her since her father left."

I grinned at her and kept shoveling the food in. "It's just so good," I mumbled, my mouth full. The chair fell over backward when I jumped up, and juice ran onto my shirt as I drained my glass.

"Since when do you love pancakes that much? Ivy Marie, what are you up to?"

I raced from the room.

"Don't you dare go swimming on that full stomach! You'll sink like a stone. And won't that be lovely. I'll have to tell your father my pancakes dragged you to the bottom. Ivy Marie!"

But I was already out the door and across the yard, racing to the beach, to my new friend at Boneyard Reef.

It was a lucky thing that a rain squall blew up, what with the stitch in my side from running on a bellyful of pancakes. By the time the rain ended, I was rested and feeling better and the cramp didn't return as I slowly swam away from shore.

I hung motionless over the reef, watching and waiting. Once, for just an instant, I thought I saw a light, but it was only a sun ray, floating down through the water like curling smoke. I waited so long, my fingers turned rubbery white and wrinkly. A school of small silver fish bubbled around my body and poked at my mask. I brushed at them lightly and stared down to where the Spanish galleon rested. I thought something moved, and I strained to see, but the bottom—usually as clear as crystal—was cloudy with shifting sand.

A large rolling wave lifted me suddenly, pulled me away from the reef, then shoved me back again. I raised my head quickly and looked around. If the sea was building, I needed to swim back to shore. But the sea was calm and shimmery. I held my breath and kicked down toward the ledge and swam through the coral where the ghost had first dropped my golden coin.

The current dragged at my feet, so strong it felt like hands were pulling me down, and I kicked angrily to escape it. My chest burned as I tried to claw my way to the surface for air. The current hugged my legs, and a mouthful of water poured into my lungs. The sea raged around and above me. For the first time ever, it became my enemy and I fought it. But it wouldn't let me go.

Desperate for air, my lungs on fire, I stretched my arm toward the light above in a last, futile attempt to save myself. Then a darkness as hard as night closed around me and I felt myself drifting weightlessly, no longer caring if I drowned. Suddenly, someone grasped both my hands and wrenched me to the surface. As I broke free, I thought I saw a huge, luminous shape hovering over the reef, heaving in a violent surf, but it turned to mist before my eyes and melted into a calm sea.

I coughed up water and swallowed great gulps of air. I called out to whoever had saved me, but no one was there. I spun around, and when I looked toward shore, I saw the girl. She was standing on the far end of the beach, staring out to sea. I called to her, but she didn't answer. She didn't even look toward me. She just stared, as if she were straining to find something on the far horizon. I looked to see what she was staring at, but nothing was there. When I looked back to her, she was gone.

I swam to shore and sat on the beach for the longest time, hugging myself and rocking. Had someone tried to kill me? Was it the ghost girl I thought would be my friend? Or was it only the current? And had I imagined someone pulling me free because I was starting to drown? I didn't know, but one thing was for sure: As I stopped shaking, I started getting mad—really mad.

Some friend she turned out to be, I thought. *Didn't even show up to help me when I almost drowned. And it was her fault I was out there in the first place.*

"Well, you can just find someone else to haunt!" I shouted. Crying in spite of my anger, I jammed my sandy feet into my sneakers and stood up on rubbery legs. "And keep your hands off my dress!"

"But where will I keep my fish?"

When I spun around, I almost bumped into her, she was standing so close to me—and wearing my very best dress.

Her eyes were the palest blue. She stopped smiling and reached up to touch my face when she saw my tears, but I pulled back and rubbed them away with the back of my hand. Then she grinned and tugged that smelly fish halfway out of the pocket of my dress. I grabbed for the pocket—ghost or no ghost it was *my* dress—and she pulled away at the same time. The pocket ripped free and hung open. But there wasn't a fish to be seen.

Neither of us moved for the longest time. We just stood there staring at the ripped pocket. Then our eyes met and she yelled, "Ha!" and turned and sprinted across the beach, laughing and calling, "Ivy Marie Bell, you couldn't outrun an old sea turtle!"

I tore after her, yelling, "That's my dress, you!"

It was like racing the wind. She laughed and laughed, a sound so sweet and light, it seemed to lift her and carry her right through the air, until she was so far beyond the beach I thought I'd lost her.

THREE

She was gone when I got to the clearing. I was slowly circling in place, thinking she might sneak up behind me, when I heard a loud trumpeting noise. Two of the largest birds I'd ever seen glided from the sky. They were some kind of crane—taller than my father even—snowy white with long black feathers edging their massive wings. I held my breath and froze in place so they wouldn't see me and fly away.

"What are you standing so still for?"

I jumped as my ghost friend sauntered past me.

"They're just birds," she said.

"Be quiet so you don't scare them away," I whispered.

She turned toward me and there was something different about her, but I didn't know exactly what it was. "Why should they be afraid of me?"

I reached out to stop her as she started moving toward them, but she wheeled away and ran toward the birds.

"Don't! You'll scare them off!" I expected them to whoosh in the air, startled by her sudden movement.

She didn't frighten them at all. And it wasn't like they didn't see her because she was a ghost and invisible. They did see her. They watched her the whole time.

When she got to them, she turned to me and stuck her hip out, as if to say "See? I told you so."

I took a step toward her and the cranes grew skittish. I stopped dead-still again. She threw her head back and laughed. And then she trumpeted, just like the cranes had done before they landed. The birds trumpeted again and started dancing, bowing and turning their long necks upside down and leaping in the air, spreading their wings out like capes. My ghost friend was leaping and dancing and honking along with them. And there I was, frozen in place, while they were all having a merry old time. The cranes took off and the air hummed as their huge wings drove up and down. They flew higher and higher, until they turned toward the sun and disappeared.

"I knew you'd scare them away," I shouted, running toward her.

She just smiled. I didn't feel like telling her it was the most beautiful thing I'd ever seen. No one had invited me to honk and dance. Besides, I still didn't know what had happened at the reef, whether someone—or something— had tried to drown me.

Her eyes darkened like she was reading my mind. All at once I realized what had seemed different about her before. Her eyes were no longer blue. They were brown like mine. And her blond hair was darker too.

"What's wrong with your eyes?"

"Nothing's wrong with them." She started blinking real fast and silly to prove it.

"They changed color. Your hair's different too."

Her brows knitted together in confusion. "So?"

"So? Well, either you have blue eyes or brown eyes. Which is it?"

She chewed on her lip, her face screwed up in a frown, like she didn't know the answer.

"Why did you change yourself?" It seemed like a stupid question, after I asked it, as if some ghost law dictates how ghosts are supposed to look.

She turned toward the horizon, searching for something, the same way she'd searched earlier. Then she stared back at me and tilted her head. Without warning, her eyes turned to blue, deep and cold. Then they changed again, lighter and lighter to cloud-gray, and then again as black as stones. All the while, she kept smiling. Her hair turned white and she pulled great clumps of it out and tossed it in the wind. It blew away like dandelion puffs. Her skin wrinkled up and turned yellow, then rubbery like an old woman's who'd been buried in water for a long time.

I backed up, my breath coming in ragged gasps. I was frightened to death, and the strange thing was, she looked frightened too, as if she had no control over what was happening. Then she turned into a regular girl again, and her brown hair grew halfway down her back like mine.

She laughed, but her voice had a quiver. "Which way do you like me best?"

She chewed on her lip, as if she were trying to decide what to do. In an instant she looked exactly like she had the first time I'd seen her up close in my yard, with long blond hair down to her waist, and the palest blue eyes.

"Why did you do that? Make yourself ugly?" I demanded.

Her eyes grew anxious, but she stuck out her chin and said, "Because I can."

My heart was knocking away and I was having a hard time holding back my tears. I wheeled around and ran.

"Wait! Ivy, please!" Her voice sounded frightened and desperate. I stopped and heard her move up behind me.

"I fixed your pocket," she said quietly. "See?"

The neediness in her voice surprised me. I wondered, *Why has she come to haunt me?* The question made me shiver.

I turned around. "What's your name?"

She looked blank.

"Your name? Don't you have a name?"

She stared into my eyes, and maybe it was the light, but her own eyes seemed to fill with tears. She touched my cheek and her hand felt as warm as sunshine. "Rose," she said.

I sucked in my breath. "That's not your name! That's my *mother's* name! You pulled it right out of my head because you don't have one of your own!"

She looked worried again and closed her eyes, like she was trying to remember something. "Eleanor?" she asked.

"Are you asking me? It's *your* name."

"My name is . . . Eleanor Moneypenny."

We stood there staring at each other, until something above my head caught the light and I looked up. A long white feather came floating down. She jumped up and snatched it out of the air.

"It's for you," she said, handing it to me.

She sprinted away and started racing toward the beach. "Ivy Marie Bell! You couldn't catch an old sea turtle!"

Clutching my feather, I flew after her, across the clearing, over the dunes. I didn't care that she was a ghost or that she might harm me. I could hear her laughter in the air, and I only cared that I finally had a friend, a friend who had given me a gold coin and a white feather. And her name was Eleanor Moneypenny.

FOUR

It didn't surprise me when Dad got word to us that he'd be gone much longer than expected. He'd done it many times before, especially in the last few years, but for the first time, it didn't bother me at all. I had Eleanor, and she was all I needed.

Every morning she met me in the yard—unless she hid first and made me search for her. Whenever she did that, I'd always feel panic, like I might never see her again. But I always found her, hiding in a tree or crouched under the trailing vines of wild roses, and we'd laugh and everything would be fine.

The only time we didn't laugh was when I'd find her on the beach, staring out to sea, because then she didn't know I was there. I raced across the sand, shouting her name, the first time I discovered her in a trance.

"Eleanor! I've been hunting all over for you! Let's look for shells." I loved to go shelling with her, because the shells she found were the most beautiful I'd ever seen, shells that must have come from the deepest ocean.

"Come on," I called.

She never even turned. She just kept staring out to sea. "What is it, Eleanor?" I asked. "What's wrong?"

She didn't seem to hear me. A breeze blew a wisp of hair across her eyes and I tried to smooth it away. Her skin felt like warm water as my hand passed through it. I yanked my hand out, startled.

"Eleanor, please look at me." My voice caught in my throat. "Please."

She turned to me and her eyes widened in surprise. "Rose," she whispered.

I stumbled back as if I'd been pushed. "It's Ivy," I said. "Ivy!"

Reaching out to touch my face, she said my mother's name again.

"Stop it, Eleanor. It's me, Ivy."

She blinked rapidly, and I knew she was returning from whatever faraway place or time she'd gone to.

"Eleanor, what are you looking for when you stare out to sea? Why did you say my mother's name?"

I thought from the look on her face that maybe she didn't answer because she didn't know. But she folded her arms across her chest and arched her eyebrows. "I never said your mother's name."

"You did too. You said, 'Rose.'"

A glimmer of recognition flashed in her eyes and then died. "I said no such thing. And stop questioning me."

"I just want to know. What are you always staring at? How come you can't even see me?"

She looked frightened by my questions, but she lifted her chin defiantly and said, "Don't be rude, Ivy Marie. It doesn't become you." Her remark sounded strange, as if she were repeating something an adult had said.

Aunt Ethel called my name from the path and I spun around in surprise. When I looked back, Eleanor was gone.

She stayed away for days, and after that I was afraid to ask her personal questions. As much as I wanted to know why she called me Rose, I couldn't ask because I was too afraid she'd go away and never come back.

When she finally returned, I woke up to find her sitting in my bed, my box of hair clips in her lap.

She frowned. "You're a mess. I'll braid your hair."
Trying to act casual, I sat up and stretched. "You don't know how to braid hair. You always wear yours down."

She narrowed her eyes. Then—*poof!*—she was gone. But she materialized again quickly, looking very pleased with herself. Our noses almost touched as she leaned in and said, "I can do *anything* I want."

She was teasing, yet a prickle of fear ran through me. Suddenly she was behind me brushing my hair. I tried to turn, wondering where she had gotten the brush, but she yanked my hair to keep me still.

"Ouch! That hurt."

"It did not. Stop fidgeting," she said crossly. After exactly one-hundred strokes, she twined her fingers through my hair and began braiding. I didn't tell her how lonely I'd been without her, because I didn't want to remind her of why she'd gone in the first place.

But I did ask, "Eleanor, where do you go when you're not with me? Do you float off like barbecue smoke?" When I giggled, she gave my hair another tug and I poked her with my elbow.

She whispered in my ear. "In the middle of the night, when you're asleep, I stand over your body and stare into your soul."

"You do not!"

"I do so! And sometimes I steal your body and walk it to the edge of the cliff and—"

I leaped off the bed.

She grinned. "Braid my hair now. And pin it on top like I fixed yours."

My fingers were clumsy, imagining her sneaking into my body, and she chuckled as if reading my mind. When I was midway through braiding her hair, she began to hum. It was a faintly familiar melody, haunting and sweet, and I closed my eyes and swayed with the sound. Eleanor stopped humming because I'd stopped working on her hair. The moment passed and I began braiding again.

We rushed to the wall mirror when I finished. Her reflection was shimmery and beautiful, but the golden braid I'd pinned on top was messy and lopsided, slipping down over one eye. I covered my mouth to keep from laughing. She got a snooty look and her image dissolved from the mirror. I was shocked at my own image, how pretty I looked, my hair perfectly in place. It gave me an old-fashioned look, like that of young women in pictures from long ago.

Something fell to the floor. When I leaned to pick up the conch shell that had fallen, it started sliding slowly across the floor, as if the snaily creature was still inside. Then all the large shells in my room began creeping around. They sucked onto the wall, slithered to the floor, and headed for my feet. I hopped around on my toes, laughing, telling Eleanor to stop, but they slid over my bare feet, wet and slimy like a long tongue. My braid fell loose, and I could hear Eleanor laughing, but she wouldn't make herself visible.

A board creaked outside the door and I knew Aunt Ethel was listening. I dove for the bed and almost landed on top of Eleanor when she suddenly materialized.

Aunt Ethel called, "What are you up to, Ivy Marie?"

Eleanor and I buried our heads under the same pillow, smothering our laughter.

The sky was cloudless and a brilliant blue, and the air smelled of mangoes. The water was calm and shimmering like green satin. I was surprised when I heard Aunt Ethel on the dock.

She looked so funny creeping nervously along that I bit the insides of my mouth to keep from laughing. Aunt Ethel had always worried that I would drown right before her eyes if she didn't reach me in time. She was still determined to overcome her fear of the shifting dock. Her legs wide apart like Frankenstein's monster, she placed one foot in front of the other, slowly, trying to keep her balance. The dock teetered and she clutched her chest. A breeze caught the edge of her faded housedress and I could see where she'd knotted her stockings just below the knees to keep them up. Aunt Ethel refused to wear long pants of any kind. She said they made women look like gangsters.

"Dad's coming back, Aunt Ethel. I can feel it."

"Now, don't be silly. He'll be back when he gets back."

But I knew he'd be home soon. Somehow, I always

seemed to know right before he came, especially when I'd started missing him the most. Then I could almost *feel* his boat turn toward Mystic Island whenever I wanted it to.

"Come back to the house, Ivy. You sit in this sun any longer, you'll burn up. Won't that be lovely? Your father comes home to a child fried to a crisp. Blisters all over you."

Eleanor was treading water, watching my aunt and me. I was surprised to see her looking so hurt, like she was jealous of my aunt's attention.

"He'll be here soon, Aunt Ethel," I said. "Any second the *Ivy Rose* will pop onto the horizon. And I'll be right here waiting, the very first thing Dad sees."

Aunt Ethel decided to humor me. "Then why in heaven's name are you fishing? Your father will have a boatload of fish." She clucked her tongue. "With those bones just waiting to stick in your throat."

I had a line tied to a willow twig that Eleanor and I had been fooling around with, pretending she was a fish that kept getting away. The line hung slack in the water.

Aunt Ethel reached a brown paper sack out to me. "Well, you better eat something so you don't starve to death."

"Thanks," I said, jumping up. "Did you bring some of those oatmeal cookies you were baking?"

"A person could end up with diabetes eating all that sugar like you do. Kidneys shut down. Bam. You're dead, just like that."

I dug around in the bag and pulled a cookie out, still warm and soft. I wasn't looking at Eleanor, but I could feel her watching us. Closing my eyes, I bit into it. "Mmmm, it's perfect." I leaned over and kissed my aunt on the cheek.

The dock tipped suddenly and Aunt Ethel lost her

footing and grabbed onto my arm. The twig flipped into the water and floated on top for a second. Then the fishing line went taut—and Aunt Ethel's face turned as white as paste. The line zinged the willow through the water like a great white shark was dragging it away.

"Oh, my heavens! Did you see that? Oh, my heavens! Get off this dock this instant! This instant!" She yanked on my arm to make me walk with her.

"It's nothing, Aunt Ethel, really. Probably just a grouper."

"Sharks! That's what's out there. I knew it!"

As I helped my aunt off the dock, I stamped roughly on the planks, hoping to clobber Eleanor one in the head for scaring Aunt Ethel like that. I noticed the knot in one of her stockings had come undone, and the stocking was sagging down her leg like a snake shedding its skin. She looked kind of funny standing there, her hair coming undone, one stocking up, one down. Still, I didn't like the idea that Eleanor had upset her. Shouldn't a ghost *know* when a person's afraid?

Aunt Ethel knew there was no point in trying to make me leave, not when I thought my father was due in, so she gave up trying. She walked back to the house, mumbling something about me being the death of her.

I stomped to the end of the dock and stood there, my fists stuck to my hips. Eleanor broke through the surface, her hair silky and wet, a big grin slapped on her face.

"Don't ever scare my aunt like that again," I said.

Her eyes turned a dark smoky blue. The water was up to her neck, her arms weaving, keeping her afloat. She glared at me.

"My father!" I yelled. "There's the *Ivy Rose!*" I jumped up and down and swung my arms over my head. "Look, there's my father!"

Eleanor turned slowly and stared at my father's boat. She turned back and watched me jumping up and down on the dock with the same jealous expression she'd had when I'd been talking to Aunt Ethel. The water began to roll under the dock, and the sea churned beyond her.

The *Ivy Rose* grew larger, like a drop of red ink on a green blotter. Suddenly, she began to roll in a building sea. One second she'd be there, then she'd disappear between the swells. I knew what was causing the sea to build so violently.

"Stop it, Eleanor," I said quietly, my eyes never leaving my father's red fishing boat. "Stop it right now."

A cloud of seagulls screeched and wheeled above the boat, drawn by the smell of fish. But the seas grew higher and the *Ivy Rose* rocked dangerously from side to side.

"Stop it now, or I'll never speak to you again." The skin got tight around my scalp as I watched my father's boat nearly capsize. "Eleanor, stop it." I looked into her brooding eyes. "Please," I whispered.

And just like that, the sea calmed. Eleanor began to laugh and squirted water on my shirt.

She seemed contrite when I didn't laugh with her. "I was only playing," she said. "Don't be mad."

The *Ivy Rose* motored up to the dock and, like always, my father was a sight—fried to a crisp, my aunt would say, but as dark as a penny from weeks in the sun. He never shaved on his fishing trips, and his beard was coal black except for the gray stripes that grew down either side of his chin. I called it his werewolf face.

He tossed the lines and I flipped them over the bollards. Before he could step off the boat, I was already in the air, springing onto the deck, shouting, "Permission to come aboard, Captain!" I landed with a thump and sea-gulls swooped into the air.

My father didn't smile at first. He stared, like seeing me was a shock. It was something he'd started doing a year or two earlier, around the time his fishing trips got longer and longer. But when I ran up to him, he wrapped his arms around me tightly. "Permission granted, Ivy."

"Dad, it got so rough. Are you okay?" I kept my face pressed against his chest.

He held me away from him and his brows curled together. "There wasn't a ripple out there, Ivy. It was smooth as glass."

Eleanor surfaced next to the boat, her eyes worried, needing to know everything was all right between us. I laughed and she smiled, then sank out of sight. I squeezed my arms around my father. I hadn't realized until that moment how frightened I had been, not only because I thought Eleanor had put my father in danger, but also because I knew I'd have to give her up forever if she ever hurt anyone I loved. And the thought of losing her was more than I could bear.

She hid from me later that day, making me search like crazy. I was relieved that she wasn't on the beach in a trance, but I started getting nervous because I didn't know where else to look. Calling her name, my toes digging into the sand, I heard her laugh overhead. And there she was, sitting crosslegged in the air.

"What are you doing up there?"

"Hanging around," she said.

"Very funny. Come on down."

But she didn't come down. She raised a conch shell to her mouth instead and started to blow. She made the most beautiful music I'd ever heard pour out of the conch horn, and I knew she was trying to make up for scaring me that afternoon. I started to twirl slowly, but the melody changed. It became faster, spinning me faster too, around and around. Dolphins began leaping out of the water, hundreds of them, diving and flying up again, hanging in the air for the briefest moment like crescent moons. Eleanor lifted me higher and higher as I spun and danced in the air. She put her arms around me and we floated down like two feathers. Breathless with laughter, we ran along the beach, our fingers twined together. It was moments like this that made me certain she'd never leave me, that we'd be together forever at the end of Mystic Island.

"Chew that fish forty times before you swallow, young lady." Aunt Ethel flaked through her plate, searching out lurking fish bones. "Might as well be eating razor blades."

"Now, Ethel, there are no bones to worry about in a fish this size. You know that." My father looked so handsome, all shaved and wearing a fresh white shirt.

"Aunt Ethel, help!" I grabbed my throat and started hacking and choking. Eleanor was watching from the window, and my death act was mostly for her benefit.

"Make jokes, go ahead." Aunt Ethel pushed her plate back. "You could drop like a stone before anyone got to do that hemlock maneuver."

"We had a good run, Ivy. One of the best," Dad said. He cleared his throat but avoided my eyes. "We'll be able to get that house one day soon. Sorry it couldn't be in time for the beginning of high school."

I said, "It's okay, Dad." And in a way, it really was. It seemed like all I had ever talked about was moving into town and going to school with other kids. Now it didn't even matter, not since Eleanor had come. She was the only friend I would ever need.

She started floating up outside the window, until only her feet were dangling in view. She knocked her toes together and fanned her feet back and forth. I couldn't help myself and started to giggle. Dad looked over his shoulder and back at me, frowning. A pan suddenly lifted off the stove by itself and began to tip over.

Before I could stop myself, I jumped up and yelled, "No! Put that down!"

"What is it, Ivy?" Dad asked quietly. Aunt Ethel's lips were pressed together tightly.

"Oh," I said, flustered. "It was a cat. At the window. I thought it was going to jump in."

Aunt Ethel stared at the window, then slid her chair back. For the first time I could remember, she left the room without saying a word.

I was surprised to see that Dad's tan had drained away. He acted like *he* had seen a ghost. He squeezed my wrist. "What's wrong, Ivy?"

"Really, Dad, it's nothing. Just a cat." I started rattling

the empty dishes in a stack, thinking I'd strangle Eleanor for making me laugh and call out. When I looked up, Aunt Ethel was in the doorway. She and my father were staring at each other, both of them pale and upset, looking like they shared some terrible secret.

FIVE

That night the dreams began.

At least I thought they were dreams. It felt like someone was holding my hand the way I imagined my mother used to do, leading me through thick fog that curled around my ankles like a wet snake. Although the path was familiar, I sensed danger and tried to turn back, but my body couldn't turn to the right or left. I struggled to wake up, but the dream wouldn't let me loose.

The fog drew me closer and closer to the edge of a cliff that overlooked Boneyard Reef. Silence wrapped itself around me as thick as the fog at my feet. I couldn't hear a sound, not even the wind that was blowing through the palm trees and whipping whitecaps across the sea. A sailing ship appeared about a mile out from the coast. It must have been heading for the deepwater harbor at the far end of Mystic Island, but it altered course and sailed straight toward Boneyard Reef.

I tried to call out to the ship, but my voice couldn't penetrate the thick air. It wouldn't have mattered, anyway. The ship was too far away for the crew to hear my warning. When it struck the reef, the wind filled the sails and dragged the ship over on its side.

I saw Eleanor on the beach, watching the empty horizon. "Eleanor," I tried to call. "Eleanor." But my throat was paralyzed and no sound came out.

Palm fronds smacked together like sharp swords. I moved toward the path that went down to the sea. I tried to run to her, but my feet dragged in the fog. One foot slipped out from under me and I fell. Then I saw a woman to my left, her long white nightgown snapping around her ankles, her dark brown hair whipping in the wind. She stood and watched Eleanor from the edge of the cliff. A terrible yearning stirred in my chest. I tried to get up from the ground and run to the woman, but I cried out in pain as my hand pressed down on something sharp. Bright red blood was seeping from a crescent-moon cut in the palm of my hand.

The smell of frying sausage wafted into my room. My stomach growled and I was surprised at how hungry I felt.

The nightmare curled around the edges of my memory. I heard my father's heavy step pass by my door and almost called to him, to tell him about Eleanor Moneypenny and my dream. But I kept silent. Did I want him to know about my friend? Did I want to share her with anyone, even my father?

I crawled out of bed and opened my bedroom door. I could hear Aunt Ethel speaking to my father, her voice an urgent whisper. I don't know why, but I knew they were talking about me. I edged down the hallway along the wall.

"It's starting all over, Albert. I can't go through this again."

"She said she saw a cat."

"What cat? There aren't any cats around here." I heard the skillet slam on the stove. "She's seeing things, just like—"

"No!" My father's anger shocked me.

"She's been acting very strange. I found her talking to someone in the yard, and a couple of times I've heard her whispering and no one was there."

"Children do that, Ethel. They have imaginary playmates." I could tell that my father didn't believe what he was saying.

"*Little* children do that. Not children Ivy's age. It's the same thing as her mother—a grown woman believing in ghosts. Rose had me a nervous wreck, Albert. Spirits jumping out of the woodwork."

"Enough! There was nothing wrong with Rose. I won't have you say otherwise."

I could hear Aunt Ethel take a deep breath. "Ivy's alone too much, Albert. This ghost business is dangerous. It killed Rose, didn't it? You have to do something about Ivy before she ends up dead like her mother!"

The hallway tilted and I was suddenly dizzy. *Dead like her mother.* A ghost had killed my mother? I leaned against the wall and tried to ease my way back to my room, my head swimming. My father and aunt were still speaking, but their words were garbled like a record played at the wrong speed. *Dead like her mother!*

I stumbled into my room and fell back against the closed door. Eleanor was staring at me from outside the window. I thought of the times she'd called me "Rose."

I ran to the window. "What happened to my mother? Did you hurt her?"

Eleanor looked confused, but tried to cover up by folding her arms across her chest.

"Don't pretend you don't know what I'm talking about. What happened to my mother? What happened to Rose?"

Eleanor's eyes got dreamy and she repeated the name, "*Rose.*"

"Yes, Rose!" I shouted. "What happened to her?"

She grew serene, closed her eyes, and started humming. Suddenly she stopped. Her body stiffened. Her eyes snapped open, dark and angry, like she'd just remembered something. She said, "Rose tried to make me go away. She wanted to send me away." Her eyes got even darker.

"And so you hurt her? She didn't die from the flu. . . . you killed her because she tried to send you away? Answer me!"

Eleanor stared at me defiantly. I couldn't tell if she was refusing to answer or if maybe she didn't know what had happened to my mother, but I was too angry and frightened to think clearly. I grabbed a box from my vanity—the scrimshaw box that held my gold coin—and flung it at her. The box bounced against the sash and onto the floor. The coin went through the window but passed right through Eleanor's body. I rushed across the room.

"Tell me what happened!" I reached out to grab her and my hands went through her body like she'd turned into mist. Eleanor looked stunned by my fury and I thought for a moment she would cry, but she got angry instead and her blue eyes turned to ice.

"Did you hurt my mother? Did you kill her?"

Her eyes became flat black stones. "She wanted to send me away."

I didn't want to believe she'd hurt my mother, but the coldness in her eyes pierced my heart like a blade. "I hate you!" I sobbed. "I hate you!" I swung my arms at her, back and forth, but they passed right through her.

It shocked me when her eyes filled with tears, but she fought back with a gust of wind that blew across my vanity, scattering everything all over my room, ribbons, shells, a small crystal ball on the end of a string. A silver hand mirror that had once belonged to my mother shattered violently against the wall, shards of glass exploding in the air. The closet door flew open and slammed back and forth— *bam, bam, bam.* My good dress blew out and fell at my feet. Buttons flew off and rolled across the floor like dried peas.

Aunt Ethel pounded on my door. "For heaven's sake, Ivy, what's all that racket in there?"

I bunched my dress in my fist and tried to catch my breath. Finally I answered, "I'm just cleaning my room."

"Well, it sounds like you're wrecking it, not cleaning it," she said through the door. "Come have some breakfast."

I wiped the tears from my face with the dress and tossed it on the shelf in my closet. I opened the door a crack. "Where's my father?"

"He took the boat into town. He unloaded the fish yesterday, but he said he needed to settle up with the crew." She tried to lean into my room to look around, but I wouldn't open the door any further. "Look at you, all pale and sweaty. Doesn't clean for months, then cleans on an empty stomach. Have your breakfast."

"I'll be right there," I said, and pushed the door shut and locked it.

I crawled through the mess on the floor, deliberately ignoring the window. My mother's shattered mirror was at my knees and I tried to piece it together, but it was hopeless. Had Eleanor ever been my friend? Or had she tried to kill me, too, that day on the reef, just like she must have killed my mother?

I started to walk to the door and hesitated. How had she even known my mother? I wondered. My throat ached from holding back my tears. I wanted to look over my shoulder to the window, but I knew there was no point. Eleanor was gone.

SIX

Aunt Ethel finally got tired of watching me rearrange the eggs and sausage on my plate and scraped the food into the trash. Cold orange juice was all I could get down. I stared at her over the rim of my glass, her arms elbow-deep in sudsy water. Several times I started to ask her what had happened to my mother, since she obviously hadn't died of the flu like I'd always thought. But I didn't want to know . . . couldn't bear to know. I thought of Eleanor's angry eyes when she'd spoken of my mother. It was clear to me she had done something to her, maybe because my mother had wanted her to go away. But how had she known my mother? And why had my mother wanted her to leave? Was it because she realized Eleanor was dangerous?

"I'm going to the beach for a while, Aunt Ethel."

"I thought you were cleaning your room. Heaven knows it could use a good cleaning." She dried her hands on a dishtowel.

"Maybe later," I said.

My voice must have sounded strange to her, because she walked across the room and pressed her damp hand against my forehead. "Well, you don't have a fever." I'm not sure what she saw in my eyes that made her say, "Go on ahead, then. The cleaning can wait."

When the screen door slammed behind me she called out, "Stay away from that reef. Remember that shark we saw dragging your fishing pole yesterday! Won't that be lovely . . . ."

I walked to the side of the house, not listening to what she said. There was no breeze, and my father's shirt hung limply on the line. I scuffed my foot through the dirt under my window, looking for the gold coin. It wasn't there. I waited, wondering if Eleanor would show up. If she did, I'd turn my back on her and walk away. No, I'd make her tell me what happened to my mother. I wasn't surprised when she didn't come.

I almost never went to the cliff that overlooked Boneyard Reef. There was a shortcut to the beach that I always took, quicker and safer than the steep path that ran down from the cliff. I felt dizzy as I crept along the same route I'd taken in my dream the night before.

When I got to the cliff, I climbed through the brush and edged out to the very spot where the woman in my dream had stood. I wondered again if the woman had been my mother. What had Eleanor done? I took several steps closer to the edge and looked down to the empty beach. *Mother,* I thought, *did she hurt you?*

For a moment I sensed my mother's presence. I imagined her watching Eleanor from this very spot and felt an ache, a longing for both of them. Suddenly, I heard men's voices, and just as suddenly, silence, like someone had turned a radio on and off. My heart hammered in my chest. Again I heard the voices, closer this time, and again they shut off.

I ran down the steep path, building up speed, trying to dig the sides of my sneakers in to slow my descent. I fell on my backside and bounced the rest of the way to the bottom.

I stumbled along the beach and crawled under a sea grape tree to hide in case anyone was following. No one came. I finally threw myself back against the cool sand.

What's wrong with me? I wondered. *Why am I imagining things that seem so real?*

My palm was throbbing. I held it in front of my face, then sat up slowly, staring in disbelief at the crescent cut in my palm. This was the cut I got in my dream! Had I actually been on that cliff, watching a ship turn into the reef? Was that really my mother staring down at Eleanor?

She was always saying my mother's name. Now she was gone, and I might never have a chance to learn the truth.

I don't know how long I lay there before I fell asleep. When I woke, it was late afternoon and the *Ivy Rose* was slipping up to the dock, towing a smaller boat behind. Sand clung to the backs of my bare legs and I brushed it off before going to meet my father. I didn't rush up to greet him like I usually did. I was angry because he and Aunt Ethel must have been lying to me for years about my mother.

My father waited, his hands stuffed in his back pockets. He looked awkward, sort of excited and nervous at the same time.

"I have a surprise for you, Ivy." He got a little flustered when I didn't answer, and he turned and walked to the stern of our boat.

"This is it," he said. "Your own boat."

I stood there speechless. It was an open wooden skiff, black with red trim, at least twenty feet long. The outboard engine was twenty-five horsepower.

I swallowed. "But, Dad, I don't need . . . I mean, it's nice, but why do I need a boat so big?" Actually, I didn't care if I had a boat at all, big or small. Most of the time when I wasn't doing schoolwork, I just read or shelled or swam the reef. Then Eleanor had come and all of my time had been spent with her.

Dad cleared his throat. "Yes, well, there's more to the surprise." He seemed relieved when Aunt Ethel came padding toward the dock.

"You're just in time," my father said, taking her elbow to steady her. "Well, here it is." He pointed to the skiff. "Ivy's new boat. So she can start school next week."

My mouth fell open. Aunt Ethel and I looked at each other, then we both turned and stared toward the distant end of the island.

My father cleared his throat. "Yes, well, it's fifteen miles to school, I know. But it's protected by reef most of the way. Unless the wind's up and the sea's breaking, it should be safe. If not, you can stay home. You've been studying at home since you started. Missing a few days of school now and then won't matter."

Aunt Ethel pressed her hand against her chest. "We'll lose her in a week. She'll sink like a stone."

"Stop it," my father said, an edge to his voice. "She's old enough to do this. She'll be fine." He jumped into the boat and it rocked. "She can handle the *Ivy Rose* almost as well as I can. This little boat will be nothing for her. You'll be in shoal water. The engine cuts out, you drop the anchor. You can't start it, you swim ashore and walk. It's good exercise. Look here, two anchors." He swung one over the side and it splashed loudly, startling a gull into the air.

"Oh, my heavens." White splotches appeared on Aunt Ethel's cheeks and she turned her face up to the sky.

"Dad, the school's around the point. Where will I dock it?"

My father scratched his head. "Okay, that might get a little tricky. You'll have to anchor out and wade to shore. Mind the tide, so you don't get left high and dry when school lets out. Your aunt will be watching for you every day while I'm away. She'll stand right here at the end of the dock."

Aunt Ethel took a couple of steps backward.

"You're all enrolled. Classes have already begun, but you can start on Monday. We need her records, Ethel. Birth certificate and shots." He breathed deeply. "But everything's done. She's going to school."

Tears stung my eyes. "I'm going to school," I murmured. Just for a moment, I forgot everything—my mother, Eleanor, the strange visions I'd started to have. Deep laughter bubbled up from my chest. I shouted, "I'm going to school!" Then I cannonballed off the end of the dock, right into the water, sneakers, clothes, and all.

At first it seemed Monday would never come. Then time whizzed by like a boat at full throttle. Dad and I had tried out the skiff together, but we'd never motored all the way to the school because I wanted to do that alone on my very first day.

Sunday night he came into my room with a big package. So many times in the past few days I'd almost asked about my mother, but a deeper place in my heart wasn't ready to hear how Eleanor might have hurt her. Even knowing Eleanor had done something to my mother, I missed her so much it was awful. But she was gone. The dreams ended, and so did the visions. I was starting school where I'd make new friends—real people who wouldn't hurt me like she had. Later, when I didn't feel so bad, I'd find out what had really happened. And maybe deep down, I thought Eleanor would come back and tell me what had happened herself.

"Well, tomorrow's the big day." The package crinkled in Dad's arms as he sat at the end of my bed.

"Yup, tomorrow. I have this feeling I'm going to walk in the classroom and Aunt Ethel is going to be standing at the blackboard. 'Well, for pity's sake, she didn't drown after all.'"

Dad smiled and shoved the package at me. He was shy about giving gifts. "Something I wanted you to have, Ivy. Just like the one I used at school."

I tore away the paper and stared at the brown leather bookbag. It was big and clunky and awful, nothing at all like what I knew the other kids would be using. I swallowed and said, "It's great, Dad. It'll keep my books nice and dry."

He pressed his hands to his knees and stood. "You're sure about tomorrow? You don't want to go in the *Ivy Rose?* I'll be home for a while longer." He avoided my eyes. "We could get you a cab from the town dock and I could—"

"Honest, Dad. I can handle it. Just like you've been telling Aunt Ethel all week."

"Your aunt's right about the life jacket. Can't hurt to wear it."

"Sure. Don't worry."

He walked toward the door and without intending to, I said, "Dad?"

"Yes?"

"Dad, do you think my mother would have liked me? The way I am today?"

He gently rubbed his forehead, covering his eyes. I'd stopped mentioning my mother to him long ago, because he always looked so pained. "Your mother . . ." He cleared his throat and went on, "You were all she ever talked about, Ivy, those last months before she . . . She wanted so much to live, to take care of you when you were a baby. We were going to buy a little house in town, just the three of us." He turned his back then and didn't speak for a moment. He kept his hand on the doorknob. "She wanted to see you grow up so much. Be there for you when you got older. She said you'd need her and . . ." His voice trailed off and his shoulders sagged.

"Yes, Ivy," he said hoarsely. "I think your mother would have liked you very much."

I almost asked him then how she had died, but he seemed so sad I didn't have the heart. He stepped out of the room without looking back.

I figured I'd never fall asleep that night, thinking about my mother and Eleanor and being so nervous and excited about my first day of school. But all of a sudden my new alarm clock was buzzing me awake like an angry hornet.

The early sky was clean and pearl-white, but the water roiled around the dock from a thrashing school of small fish. I'd once told Aunt Ethel they could be piranha and if you fell in they'd suck your bones clean just like that. She looked like she'd turned to stone, standing in the dead center of the dock afraid to move.

"It's okay, Aunt Ethel. They're harmless jacks." I stood in the skiff and tugged at the life jacket. "I feel like a big fat pumpkin in this thing."

"Tell her not to take it off till she gets to school, Albert."

"Don't take it off till you get to school, Ivy." Dad winked and I yanked on the starter cord. The engine roared to life.

I couldn't believe it when Aunt Ethel folded her hands across her stomach and started singing, her voice thin and wobbly, "School days, school days, dear old golden-rule days . . ."

Honestly, it was so corny it almost made me cry. I motored away from the dock. When I turned, my father and Aunt Ethel were watching me, the two of them standing there like wooden soldiers. I waved, revved up the engine, and started off for my first day of school.

The rising sun turned the smooth water into a flat silver platter. There wasn't a ripple inside the reef that runs the whole length of Mystic Island. I was tempted to slip off the life jacket, which was digging under my chin, but fifteen miles seemed a long way from home. I looked off to the deserted beach where Eleanor had stood when she searched the horizon, then up at the cliff, where the woman had stood watching her. Two tiger rays glided out of the water and into the air, side by side, and my throat tightened as I saw them together. They smacked down and shattered the calm silver surface.

When I worked my way around the point to the small cove where I'd anchor the boat, I got nervous in spite of my excitement.

Well, this is it, I thought, and turned the bow toward shore. Once the water seemed shallow enough, I set the anchor and bunched my skirt. As soon as I slid over the side, I realized my terrible mistake.

The water rushed above my waist. I lost my footing and dropped my shoes. Like a fool, I bent to scoop them up and soaked my hair and the front of my blouse.

"Oh, no," I cried, staring down at myself. I started to cry and punched the hull of the boat.

"Well, there's no point in leaving it here," I said out loud, and towed the boat closer to shore until the water was below my knees. I dragged my bookbag out and kicked through the surf to shore.

The sun wasn't high enough to dry my clothes even a little before I got to the school. I tried to smack the wrinkles out of my skirt from where I'd wrung it out, but it still looked like I'd slept in it overnight. I pulled on a sweatshirt to hide my wet blouse. I'd forgotten a comb, so I ran my fingers through my hair, but I just knew it looked tangled and ugly.

The school was a small one-story, red-brick building. The corridor, lined with metal lockers, smelled like egg salad and dirty sneakers. A custodian directed me to the classroom door. I knocked and waited. I knocked again and the door was swung open by a tall girl with frizzy red hair, gray fish eyes, and a mouth with lips like two dead herrings—a mouth that fell open when she looked me over.

She turned to the teacher. "Miss Lowell, I think something just washed up from the beach."

Laughter rippled through the class, and my face burned with shame. I wanted to sock her in the mouth, but I figured it wouldn't do to get expelled my very first day.

"Stop it, Sharon! Take your seat." Miss Lowell started to ask what had happened, then stopped abruptly. Seeing the look in my eyes, she smiled kindly.

"You must be Ivy, the new student. Say hello, class."

Class didn't make a sound. I walked into the room, feeling like a gawky shorebird, my shoes going *squish, squish, squish.* My wet skirt began to creep up and I had to yank it down. A boy snickered and hid his face behind his book when Miss Lowell glared at him.

"Did she *swim* here?" Sharon asked in a whisper I was meant to hear.

Miss Lowell directed me to an empty seat at the end of Sharon's row. My bookbag was as wide as the aisle and I had to turn sideways, but I still managed to whack into every knee I passed. Sharon grunted like I'd broken her leg. I was sorry I hadn't.

Miss Lowell folded her hands in front of her stomach like Aunt Ethel had done and I thought she was going to burst into song. She said, "Ivy Marie Bell, welcome to Randall Pratt School."

"*Ivy Marie Wetbottom,*" Sharon whispered.

Miss Lowell rapped her ring on top of her desk to stop the few kids who laughed.

"Now, Ivy, I'm sure we'd all like to hear something about you."

Every head in the room swiveled my way. I closed my eyes and wished I were dead.

SEVEN

It was the longest and most horrible day of my life. I felt like a freak leaving school, all wrinkled and sloppy, and Sharon had made sure I noticed my skirt was longer than any other girl's. My clunky bookbag, filled with my new books, knocked against my leg, while the other kids carried books in their arms or in canvas backpacks. They piled into their parent's cars, and some walked together, laughing and fooling around, to nearby homes. They were all so busy talking among themselves, not one person thought to say good-bye to me, which suited me just fine.

As soon as I was out of their sight I started to run to the cove, and my skiff, and home. That was all I wanted to do. Go home. I would never set foot in a classroom again. I would *never* live in that stupid town!

When I got to the edge of the shore, I swung my bookbag by its stupid leather handle and flung it as far as I could. The tide had gone out and my boat was lying in the wet sand, tipped over on its side like a beached whale.

I stamped my foot and a gray crab scurried into a bubbling hole. That's just how I felt—like an ugly old thing dodging big feet.

The sky turned blood red with sunset before the

water rose high enough to rock the boat. But it still wasn't deep enough to float me free. A horn tooted in the distance. My father rounded the point in the *Ivy Rose*. He tossed me a line and towed the skiff into deep water. If my face looked anything like the way I felt, it must have been what wiped the smile off my father's face.

"Figured the tide got you when you didn't show." He helped me onto the *Ivy Rose*. "Well, don't feel bad. It's happened to me. Isn't a sailor out there who hasn't been grounded at least once. They're lying if they say otherwise."

My teeth clenched, I said, "I'm never going back there."

He must have sensed there was more amiss than just the tide. "It was only your first day, Ivy. School can be like that. It'll get better."

I turned my head and said very quietly, "It won't get better for me because I'm never going back." We didn't speak the rest of the way home.

My aunt was waiting at the door when I raced passed her, my father right behind me. I didn't even look at her when I shouted, "I hope you didn't burn those home-schooling books, Aunt Ethel. We'll be needing them." I stormed into my room and slammed the door.

A few moments later, my father tapped on the door and opened it.

"What happened to my mother?" I demanded. "How did she die? I want to know!"

He looked like he'd been hit in the stomach. I was as shocked as he was that the question had flown out of my mouth.

"You know how she died. She had the flu," he answered.

"That's a lie!"

"Ivy, what's wrong with you?"

"She was killed. I heard you and Aunt Ethel talking."

Aunt Ethel stepped into the room, a towel twisted in her hands.

"How did my mother die?" I pressed my fingers against my lower lip to make it stop trembling.

"It was the flu," Aunt Ethel said.

"No!" I shouted.

"Yes," my father said. "It was the flu. But we found her on the path going up to the cliff. That's the only part we didn't tell you. She was delirious and walked in her sleep. The doctor said she might have died a day or so earlier from going outside, but she would have died, anyway. What's this about, Ivy?"

"You talked about a ghost," I said, "you and Aunt Ethel the other morning. I heard you."

My father looked up angrily at my aunt. She said, "Your mother thought she was talking to a ghost. It started after she had gotten pneumonia the year before. She was weak, getting sick all the time after that, which is why I came to stay. And I'd hear her talking to someone. But it wasn't a ghost. It was all in her mind."

"What was the ghost's name?" I asked in a quiet voice.

My aunt's eyes widened anxiously. "Name? There was no name, for pity's sake. It wasn't a real ghost!" She tried to hide her own doubt, but it flickered in her eyes.

I sat on the bed and my father sat beside me. "She left the house because she was sick. She was very agitated at the end, feverish. Pneumonia twice. Then the flu. She thought she had to do something. She kept saying there wasn't enough time." He sighed. "She must have climbed from the window, and being so sick, I guess she just collapsed on the path."

Aunt Ethel said, "Your father wanted to carry her back to the house. But she was delirious and tried to get away. She kept saying she had to get back to the cliff. It was the fever talking."

My father pressed his fingers against his eyes. "I think she knew all year she was going to die. Maybe that's why she started imagining things." The tone of his voice changed and I got the strange feeling he was hiding something.

"So a ghost didn't *do* anything to her?" My head was reeling in confusion. "A ghost didn't hurt her?"

Aunt Ethel walked to the door. "Ghosts? Where do you get these ideas? It was all in her head. Well, it's a good thing you got her in school, Albert. Alone too much, this is what happens. Just like her mother."

My father gave Aunt Ethel a dark look and she stopped speaking.

"I'm not going back," I said. "I hate it."

Aunt Ethel raised her eyebrows at my father and from the way he stared back at her, I knew there was no way I was getting out of it. She turned and left the room.

"Dad, wait."

He paused at the door.

"Did my mother ever say anything to you about a ghost?"

He didn't say a word for the longest time, like he was trying to decide how to answer.

"Dad?" I repeated.

He took a deep breath. "Once, when we were looking at a house in town, she said she needed to tell me something. She said . . . she told me she had a ghost friend."

He rubbed his hand across his forehead, hiding his eyes. "She wanted to tell me about it, but I laughed and told her not to be foolish." His voice broke. "I laughed at her. She didn't seem feverish that day, but I guess she must have been. But what difference did it make whether she was feverish or not?" I could tell he was speaking to himself now. "She wanted to tell me something and I laughed at her. And then something happened in front of the house we were looking at."

I whispered, "The house with the jasmine?"

"Jasmine?"

"Never mind. What happened?"

"I don't know," he answered. He seemed dazed, trying to remember. "She became upset, like she'd seen a vision. It was something about you that upset her." So quietly that I could barely hear him, he said, "She was holding you in her arms and made me promise to be a good father, to take care of you." He looked at the floor, avoiding my eyes, like he knew he'd broken his promise to my mother. He turned his back to me and said, "She died soon after that."

"Dad," I said, thinking of the woman on the cliff. "You never saved me a single picture. I don't even know what my mother looked like."

He stared over his shoulder in surprise, with that same look I'd begun to notice a year or two earlier, when his fishing trips began getting longer. His voice was barely a whisper. "She looked just like you, Ivy. Just like you."

Late that night I stood alone at my bedroom window. The air smelled of after-rain, dark and earthy. Nothing made any sense. If they'd been friends, why had my mother wanted to send Eleanor away? What had my mother seen in front of that house? Tears welled in my eyes. Eleanor had never hurt my mother; she had been her friend, just as she was *my* friend, my only friend. And I had driven her away forever.

"Eleanor," I whispered, "I'm sorry. Please come back."

The silence was as still as death.

All that week she didn't come, and school didn't get one bit better. As I motored there in the skiff on Friday morning, the early sky was snail-gray and empty. My eyes were swollen and my face felt puffy from lack of sleep. I'd tried to will myself to dream of Eleanor all night, just to be near her because I missed her so much, but thinking of her had only kept me awake. And when I had slept, it was as if she refused to visit my dreams just as she refused to come back. When I anchored the boat in the cove, something jumped in the water near the stern. I turned slowly, hoping Eleanor would be swimming around, smiling, happy to see me. Of course, she wasn't there. It must have been a ray or a big fish.

Students were giving the oral reports that had been assigned on my first day of school and Miss Lowell called on me. Every head turned. I had spent so much time worrying about Eleanor that I hadn't done the assignment. I was about to admit it when Sharon whispered to her friend, "I bet it will be about *swimming* to school."

I stomped to the front of the room without a single idea of what I would say, but I knew whatever it was, it would be better than anyone else's stupid report. I blurted out, "My report is on the ghost of Boneyard Reef."

There was dead silence, and then everyone cracked up. Only they weren't laughing *with* me, because I wasn't laughing one bit.

I took a deep breath and began. "The ghost appears only to those who have the mark. This mark." I held up my hand to show them the crescent scab that had formed over my cut. "Or to those it's going to *kill*." I glared at Sharon. "It walks the beach, moaning and wailing, crying for revenge. Back and forth, back and forth."

Miss Lowell cleared her throat slightly, and the students looked at each other and rolled their eyes. Suddenly, the door slammed shut and everyone jumped. A little thrill ran down my spine. I had been the last one to enter the room and I *knew* I had closed the door tightly.

"The ghost is angry, but no one knows why. It lures ships onto Boneyard Reef and destroys them. It climbs into the bones of sailors and stalks the decks of new ships. Survivors have said they heard bones rattle just before they struck the reef."

A light tapping came from behind the world map standing in the corner of the room—the map in front of the skeleton Mr. Gerber used in biology. Miss Lowell squirmed in her seat. The rattling got louder behind the map, which suddenly rolled up in a loud snap. The skeleton clacked and swayed. Some kids screamed, while others laughed nervously.

My voice rose. "Just before the ships hit the reef, the wind begins to howl and rain pours down like hailstones."

The windowpane rattled loudly as driving rain slashed across it. Dark leaves blew against the glass like hungry bats.

Sharon jumped up. "Miss Lowell, do you want me to shut the window the whole way?" Without waiting for an answer, she busy-bodied over, pushed it down the last two inches, and turned away. The window slid up on its own and buckets of rain poured in and soaked Sharon's back from head to foot. Her mouth dropped open and she stood there staring at the puddle under her feet.

"Miss Lowell!" she wailed.

Then a voice whispered in my ear, "*Sharon Wetbottom*," and I squeezed my eyes shut to hold back the tears.

I raced to the shore after class, ignoring the kids who stared as I flew by. I didn't care how foolish I looked, a fisherman's daughter with her skirt too long, lugging a clunky bookbag. I hit the sand still running. And there was Eleanor, sitting in my skiff, her legs crossed and her arms folded—and the boat high and dry.

I dropped the bag and tried to catch my breath. I stuck my fists on my waist. "Very funny. This boat was anchored just where it was supposed to be. You put it right back where it was."

"Make me," she said.

We just stared at each other and I started walking toward her on the hard wet sand. I was halfway to the boat when she grinned and made the tide turn and rush in. I yelped and ran backward, but it caught up to me, soaking my shoes and socks and the edge of my skirt. Eleanor was laughing, and she made me laugh, too. I made my way out to her slowly, my clothes weighing me down, the school-bag balanced on my head, and pulled myself into the boat. She put her arms around my waist and rested her head on my shoulder as I hugged her tightly.

That's how we were that afternoon, like she had never been away, and would never leave me again.

EIGHT

Dad had secured a wooden chair for Aunt Ethel at the edge of the dock. It faced the school end of the island so she could watch me going away in the morning and coming home again in the late afternoon. I could see her waving that dishtowel over her head a mile away.

It's a good thing she was sitting too. I came in so fast I whacked against the dock and rocked it. Of course Eleanor had to get theatrical and pretend I'd knocked her overboard. She disappeared under the boat. Aunt Ethel was gripping the armrests of her new chair, but when she saw the smile on my face, I guess she forgot to stay scared.

"Well, look at you now," she said. "I'm so used to seeing Miss Glumface, I'd hardly recognize you. I told you, didn't I? You just elbow your way into those cliques. *Elbow* like I did when I was in school." She poked her elbows in and out from her body and looked like a bird trying to take off. "You just push your way into those little groups and *make* people like you. That's my motto."

"You were sure right about that, Aunt Ethel." I tossed my bookbag onto the dock and climbed up after it. I had changed into my gym uniform, so she wouldn't see the sopping clothes I'd stuffed into my bag.

"It's just too bad your father didn't see that smile on your face before he left this morning."

"He went away so soon," I said.

"Well, he wants to get you that house in town. And don't go saying you don't want a house anymore. She changes her mind like the wind," she muttered.

"Aunt Ethel, Dad's never going to buy us a house. I think he wants to stay here forever, which is fine with me. Do you think it's because of Mom, like maybe her memory is here or something? Or he doesn't want to live in a new house without her?"

Something he had said the other day was nagging at me, but I pretended it didn't bother me as I asked casually, "Do you think he goes away so much because I started to look like my mother and he just can't stand seeing me anymore?"

My aunt's face softened. Then she clucked her tongue. "Is this what they teach you in school? Psychology nonsense? Well, it doesn't happen to be my business to read other people's minds, young lady. And you might take a lesson from that."

I helped her up from the chair. As we started toward shore, Eleanor glided into the air. Her eyes were closed and she was flapping her elbows like my aunt had done.

"Well, now what's so funny all of a sudden?"

"Oh, nothing, Aunt Ethel. I was just thinking of something funny that happened at school today."

"See, now that's good. Focus on the good things at

school. Keep your mind off the bad things, for pity's sake. That's the answer."

Eleanor splashed down behind us so hard the water sprayed our backs. Aunt Ethel went rigid like it was a killer whale or something.

I said, "You're right, Aunt Ethel. We have to focus on the good things." We walked off the dock together as Eleanor shot a stream of water right into the back of my head.

I raced to the beach to meet her as soon as I could get away. I hadn't mentioned it to Aunt Ethel, but the second my father returned, I planned on convincing him to take me out of school. Home-schooling would give me more time with Eleanor. We strolled the length of the beach together, holding hands and gathering shells for my collection: small periwinkles, tiny pink clam shells, even some moon-white sand dollars and green sea urchins.

I wanted so much to ask Eleanor about my mother. Had she really known her? What had she been like? What had happened between them? But I was afraid she'd get upset by my questions and go away.

The sky had seemed gray and dreary when Eleanor was gone, but now that she was back, the setting sun turned the clouds a glowing gold. They floated low above a turquoise sky with little wrinkles of peach and rose. The sea soaked up the sky and watercolors swirled across the top. Even the air smelled sweet, like summer fruit. I couldn't bear to ask any questions that might make her leave me again.

I ran into the water to get a feather floating on the surface, and when I walked back, she was gazing off toward the sea, beginning to get distant and apart from me. I slipped my arm through hers and it passed right through her body.

"Eleanor," I said. "Eleanor, come back."

She blinked and looked around and then smiled as if nothing had happened.

I took her hand and she had substance again. I said, "Eleanor, sometimes I wish you were real." I kicked at the sand and hooked my toe into a morning glory vine.

She turned and stared at me. "Real? I *am* real."

"No, I mean like me. Instead of being a ghost."

Her eyes went blank. "I'm not a ghost."

"You are too!"

"I am not!" She swung her arm at my chest and it passed right through my body like I was a fountain of water. "*You're* the ghost," she said.

Her powers made me shiver. "Very funny." I pinched a fold of skin on my arm. When I let it go, the mark was white and puffy like the sandy ring around an ant hill. I stuck my arm in her face. "See that? *That's* a pinch mark. You get them when you're *real*."

She folded her arms across her chest, so I did the same thing. We stood like that, neither one of us giving in. And that's how Aunt Ethel found me. Standing on the beach, glaring into thin air.

"For pity's sake! It's getting dark and your dinner's ready," she called to me. "I thought I heard you talking down here." She looked nervous, like maybe I was going crazy and seeing things after all, like she thought my mother had done.

"I wasn't talking," I said.

She clutched a piece of apron in her fist. "Ivy Marie, I'm sure I heard your voice."

I walked up to her and said, "Oh, yeah, I was practicing a speech for next week. That's what you heard."

"Well, come up to the house. Your food's getting cold."

I looked back and Eleanor was gone from the spot. She was standing at the other end of the beach, watching the horizon. Only this time she wasn't on the sand, she was standing in the water up to her ankles and from a distance she looked airy, like a patch of cloud that could blow away with the slightest puff of wind.

That night I lay in bed looking at the starry sky. A red star glittered like a glowing eye watching me from afar. I was drifting off when I thought I saw a pearly shimmer outside my window. I tried to wake myself, but instead I slipped into a deep dream. Angry voices nicked at my sleep—men's voices, sharp like glass breaking outside my window. I heard a shout, and then silence.

I slept deeply again. When I opened my eyes, I was standing outside my bedroom window, but as I looked back into my room, I saw myself sleeping in the bed. I had somehow left my body. I was filled with dread and tried to get back, to crawl inside myself before it was too late, but something damp and spidery dragged across my face like a sticky web in a dusty cellar. I smacked it away and Spanish moss clung to my wrist.

When I finally pulled free, I was on the path climbing toward the top of the point, wrapped in a shroud of silence. Trees shook and leaves skittered through the air like sparrows, but I could hear nothing. My bare feet could barely move through the curling fog. I put one foot in front of the other like I was fighting an undertow.

I saw the woman in the white nightgown first. Could she be my mother? She was shivering, her hands clutching her upper arms, watching the beach below. She tried to speak and I leaned toward her to pluck even the tiniest sound of her voice from the air. I couldn't hear a whisper. I tried to leave the path to go to her, but the fog pressed around my ankles like deep wet sand. Men's voices broke through the silence. An orange light flickered and went out, leaving darkness behind.

When I finally reached the top of the hill, I saw Eleanor below, alone on the beach, standing in water up to her knees. She was looking out to sea. A far-off sailing ship altered course. Its red sails snapped against a tar-black sky. It was dead on course for Boneyard Reef.

But Eleanor wasn't watching the ship. She was staring, as always, toward an empty edge of sea. The ship stayed on its new course as if something were luring it onto the reef. Was this the shadowy image I had seen looming over the reef when I almost drowned? When the ship struck, the sails shook and tore away. The ship rolled on its side, lifting and writhing like an injured whale. The woman in white was staring intently at Eleanor.

I opened my mouth to call to her—"*Mother*"—but the word couldn't pass my lips. I tried to move toward her and something snagged my ankle, pulling me to the ground and into an empty well of sleep.

My chest was catching at a sob when I came awake the next morning. I sat up, my face still wet with tears as if I had only just then been dreaming. Eleanor was standing outside my window. The early morning light bathed her in a silvery gray so pale she looked like she was fading away. I thought about my nightmare, then stared down at the long piece of ragged vine wrapped around my ankle. It trailed across my white sheet like a crack across my mother's mirror, and I knew it had not been a dream.

I slipped from the house before Aunt Ethel got up and searched the yard for Eleanor. When I couldn't find her, I ran to the beach. She was standing in water up to her knees just as I had seen her in my strange vision. She didn't answer when I called. She never answered when I found her like that, lost and waiting, staring off at the distance. I stepped close and blew softly across her cheek. Her image stirred like the surface of a bay when a leaf sets down gently. But she didn't acknowledge my breath or my presence. "Eleanor," I whispered.

I followed her eyes and stared at the emptiness beyond. A sickening thought came into my mind, a suspicion I'd tried to suppress since the first day I'd seen Eleanor on the beach watching the horizon. Had Eleanor died in a shipwreck? Is that why she was always looking out to sea? But she never even looked at the ship I saw crashing on the reef. Was she waiting for her own ship, I wondered, a ship that would never come? But that made no sense. Why was there more than one ship?

I reached up to push the hair back from her face, but she stirred like a breeze on sunlit water, and my hand passed through her body. I said her name over and over, trying to lure her back. I looked across the horizon and was shocked at how *glad* I was to see the empty sea—glad her ship could never come back and take her away from me.

She turned slowly and glared at me. Her blue eyes sharpened, scraped at my mind like flint against stone. I knew she was reading my thoughts and could tell how glad I was that she could never go away.

Her body stiffened and then something took control of her like it had once before. The pupils rolled into the back of her head and the whites of her eyes looked like swollen mushrooms. She opened her mouth and let out a shrill sound like an infant's wail. Her head flew back and she shook it wildly, trying to break free of something. But she couldn't break loose. She ripped her hair out in clumps till her scalp was bald and bloody. She flailed her arms and threw the matted snarls of hair in my face, like I was supposed to see them, feel them, understand something I was incapable of comprehending. They floated into the water and writhed like nests of eels before melting away to nothing.

"Stop it!" I screamed. "Stop it this very minute!"

She shook her fists at me like she wanted to show me the torn tufts of hair and bits of flesh she clutched. I realized in horror how much she looked like the drowned image I'd seen that first time she'd come to me underwater at the reef. Then she leaned her face close to mine and opened her dark, swollen mouth.

"*Rose,*" she hissed.

Bile filled my throat and my stomach churned as my mother's name spilled from her mouth. I shoved my hands against her chest to push her away, but I fell through her body facedown in the water near her feet. I scrambled to shore on my hands and knees.

What if Eleanor *had* killed my mother? I ran to get as far away from her as I could. Aunt Ethel and my father said a ghost hadn't harmed my mother, but since they didn't believe in ghosts, of course they would say that. Eleanor had said my mother wanted to send her away, so maybe my mother had known how dangerous Eleanor was. Is that why she'd tried to pull me away when I first saw the gold coin? Was my mother making Eleanor turn ugly to warn me?

I fell on my knees at the other end of the beach. Eleanor was waiting for me, just standing there on top of the water as if nothing had happened. She flipped a bright orange conch shell from hand to hand. It was one I didn't have in my collection, with a long pointy spiral and a mother-of-pearl flare. She was smiling.

Her eyes clouded when she realized I was crying. She came to me and knelt in the sand.

"Eleanor," I said. "Eleanor, did you . . ."

Before I could finish, she leaned over and kissed my cheek. I was faint with fear and confusion and dropped my head on her shoulder. She couldn't have hurt my mother, I thought, willing myself to believe it. She was her ghost friend. My father had said so. She must have loved my mother. Just as she loved me. I wrapped my arms around her waist and held her fiercely. I never wanted to believe anything so much in my life.

"Come on," she said, "walk out on the water with me." She ran ahead with the orange conch. "Don't be afraid. I'll make the water hold you up."

She stood on the water, tossing the shell really high, and bobbled it when it came down. It broke through the water like through a thin crust of ice, and I took a step backward, afraid to follow her.

She scooped the shell out of the water. "Well, what are you waiting for? If you want the shell, you have to come and get it."

I couldn't resist her playful smile and stepped on the surface of the water and tested it. It was rubbery beneath my feet like the skin on old Jell-O. I didn't want to walk out on the water, still afraid deep down she might hurt me, but I couldn't stop myself. I followed because I needed to prove to myself I trusted her.

As I got close, she held the shell out to me. When I reached for it, she laughed and ran off. I ran right after her, pushing my fear away. We bounced across the surface of the bay like astronauts on the moon. I started to laugh and sprang up and down on the water as she ran ahead.

She turned and stared. I recognized that jealous look on her face. I'd seen it before when she thought I was losing interest in her. Then the water started to crack. It shattered into a web of tiny lace threads and parted under my feet. I plunged in over my head. When I surfaced, I pulled a mouthful of air into my lungs. Eleanor was treading water beside me, grinning like it was a big joke.

"Bet you can't beat me!" she yelled. I looked to shore and my heart thrummed in my ears when I realized how far from land I'd run. She took off, laughing and splashing. I swam toward shore, trying not to panic. I held my head as high above water as I could, afraid that somehow a skin of ice might close over the surface and trap me below.

I staggered out of the water and fell to my knees, exhausted and out of breath. The two of us, wet and ragged, looking like lost souls that had washed out of the sea.

"I'll find you another shell," she said. "One even prettier." Then she squirted a jet of water into the air and laughed, like she didn't even know she had put me in danger—or didn't care.

NINE

There must have been winds very high up, because there wasn't a single cloud, and the horns on a sliver of crescent moon were sharp and clear against the night sky. I thought of the weather proverb my father had taught me: "Sharp horns on the moon threaten high winds."

I hoped it would blow hard by morning, so I wouldn't have to go to school and could spend the whole day with Eleanor. My new shells were lined up along the windowsill, and the long white feather Eleanor had given me when we first met was sticking out of a hole in one of them. Heavy wings beat through the air in the yard and left an echoing chord. I couldn't see the bird, but it sounded very large, and a little shiver passed through my body.

I climbed into bed with a stack of magazines, relieved that the rest of my afternoon with Eleanor had been easy and fun, but still unsettled by what had happened. I didn't let myself acknowledge the nagging fear that Eleanor could have harmed my mother or could even hurt me. I was almost afraid to remember how happy it made me to know she was a ghost and could never leave me. Could she read my mind when she wasn't there? The only thing I knew for certain was that we couldn't change the past. So Eleanor had to have died and would always be a ghost— my ghost, and my friend.

Aunt Ethel elbowed my door open and bustled in with her arms full of clean laundry. "Can't have her going to school looking like a rag picker. Not that she'd mind any, that's the sad truth." She put down some folded clothes and carried others to the closet.

"You'll have raccoon eyes if you don't put away those silly magazines and get to sleep. Skin-and-bone models. Teenage romance." She clucked her tongue. "Romance is the last thing a young girl needs, mark my words. There's enough of *that* business later on." Aunt Ethel gave me a look like she was waiting for me to sneak off to Hollywood with a total stranger.

She bent down for a fallen hanger and cried out. "Ivy Marie Bell! How could you be so careless?" Aunt Ethel picked up my mother's shattered mirror, her hand against the glass to keep the pieces from falling out. She pried slivers free from the silver frame and dropped them in the wastebasket, muttering under her breath, "Careless like her mother."

"It was an accident, Aunt Ethel. What do you mean about my mother? How was she careless?"

"Lost the matching brush, didn't she? Took it right out of this house and we never found it again after she died."

"I didn't know the mirror was part of a set." I remembered Eleanor brushing my hair. Had she taken my mother's brush?

I slipped off the bed to help my aunt with the broken glass.

"Stay! Stay! Don't put one foot on this floor!"

"Aunt Ethel, how come you didn't like my mother?"

"Didn't like your . . . what a thing to say to your own aunt, didn't like your mother! I never said a thing like that in my life. Why, I thought the world of your mother."

"Well, you thought she was kind of crazy."

"All the more reason to like her, poor thing. Talking to herself all the time." Aunt Ethel finished prying the last of the glass from the mirror. She blew out a puff of air. "She was never the same after she went into town to look at that house with your father. Came home all worried and nervous, talking to herself, talking to spirits." She put her hand on her hip and frowned at me. "Spirits who weren't there," she added.

"What was it about the house, Aunt Ethel?"

"I don't know. Something about you. But it was all in her mind. There's only one thing I'm sure about, Ivy Marie Bell. Your mother certainly loved you. I never saw the likes of it, the way she held you in her arms from morning to night. She thought the sun and the moon set by you. Why, your name was the very last thing to cross her lips."

"My name?"

"Your father lifted her right into his arms to carry her back to the house. She was out of her mind with fever, of course, kept trying to get back to the cliff to do something. 'Tell Ivy I'm sorry.' That's what she said. 'Tell Ivy I'm sorry.'"

"Why would she say that?" I asked. "What was she sorry about?"

"She was sorry to die, I guess. She loved you so much

she was sorry to die." She lifted the wastebasket and rattled the glass. "We never did find that brush, and now we don't even have the mirror. I hope they teach you to be a little more careful with personal possessions in that school of yours."

She scooped up the magazines, but I'd already slipped one under the covers. "They certainly haven't taught you anything about good reading habits. We read classics in my day, no matter how boring they were. We were taught responsibility, I can tell you that."

"Good night, Aunt Ethel."

"Hmmpf." She planted a kiss on my head and swept from the room with the clinking basket.

It was late, but still I flipped through the magazine. I suppose I was putting off going to sleep, afraid of what might happen, what I might see. Finally, unable to concentrate and thinking about how much my mother loved me, I tossed the magazine on the floor. Eleanor's smiling face came into my mind, but when I imagined her arms around me, I was suddenly ashamed. I had let a ghost become more important to me than my own mother. I had to find out what really happened. But what would Eleanor do if I insisted she tell me the truth? Would she hurt me? Would she go away and never come back? It didn't matter what she might do. I knew I would have to confront her in the morning.

As soon as I'd made my decision, I thought I saw someone pass by my window. I got up and looked out. Eleanor was gliding through the yard.

I stared after her as she made her way toward the path I'd seen my mother on. She stopped once and turned back. I thought she was waiting for me. And yet I could tell she was sightless, as if some force were moving her and wanted me to follow. Was it my mother? I didn't want to follow Eleanor that night, knowing she had the power to harm me, but no matter what it might cost me, I had to know the truth.

I climbed through the window and ran after her. The air felt strange, but I could feel my body and knew I was present in my own time. I hadn't left my body behind like before.

Eleanor left the path and glided through the thick underbrush. She entered a clearing I'd never seen. Thick limbs strangled by grasping vines reached across the clearing, forming a canopy that hid the sky. She walked straight toward the cliff and stepped over the edge.

"Eleanor!" I raced to the spot where she'd disappeared. Even knowing she was a ghost, I expected to see her body lying crumpled on the rocks below. But she was standing on a ledge that protruded from the cliff, looking up at me. Then she passed through the wall of rock and was gone.

"Where are you, Eleanor?" I looked down at the white waves crashing on the rocks and stepped back. She didn't answer my calls and I knew I'd have to follow. The ledge she'd dropped onto had a flat surface. I didn't know if it would hold my weight or whether it was wide enough for me to land on, but I got ready to jump, knowing I'd smash on the rocks below if I lost my footing. I don't know what brought me to my knees to feel for a handhold, something to help me climb down safely. My hand touched a heavy braided root and I grasped it in my fist, found another root just like it, and lowered myself over the cliff.

Hanging there by both arms, praying I hadn't misjudged my position, I dropped into the air, landing on the shelf with more room than I expected. The face of the cliff was covered with rough tangled vines, which I parted. There was Eleanor, shimmering in the darkness, standing in the center of a cave.

"Eleanor," I whispered. My voice echoed back, *Eleanor, Eleanor.*

I made my way to her slowly in the darkness, afraid of stirring the bats I pictured hanging from the dank walls. Eleanor always lost her substance when she was like this, and I couldn't bear to touch her, to feel the emptiness, to know I was all alone in this deathly place.

Her radiance was the only light in the cave and I stood close to her. "Eleanor, please be with me," I whispered. "I'm scared."

I was standing there hugging my arms when a narrow stain of light spilled across the floor. It spread like melting butter as a brilliant beam filtered down from above a crumbling stone stairway and bathed the room in light. I looked up at a full yellow moon hanging in the sky above an opening in the stone ceiling. The moon hadn't been full when I left my room. It had been a crescent moon, the horns sharp against a cloudless sky. Now the whole cave was awash with moonlight.

Someone had spent time in the cave. It looked cozy and lived in. I walked to a rocking chair in the corner. An infant's wooden cradle rested beside it. A blanket, yellowed with age, draped over the side. I pushed the chair with a finger and it rocked slowly.

I turned back to Eleanor and was surprised to see her staring at me. She looked frightened and confused, and I knew she was out of her trance.

"Eleanor, what's going on? Why are we here?"

Her eyes filled with uncertainty, and when she didn't answer, I said, "You should know, Eleanor. You're a ghost."

She tilted her chin defiantly, masking her limitations and said, "We're here because . . . because we're here. That's why."

"Oh, *great*, Eleanor. That explains everything."

A girl's laughter echoed in the cave. Then another girl began giggling, the two of them sounding much like Eleanor and me. Their images glimmered for a moment, showing them holding hands. Their faces were too elusive to make out, but I assumed it was meant to be Eleanor and me. Their shapes glittered like gold dust in a stream and faded away.

Someone hummed softly. Particles of light sparkled and became a woman sitting near the table, braiding the hair of a girl my age. She was humming to herself, that same familiar melody Eleanor had hummed when she'd brushed my hair once. I couldn't make out their faces in the golden dust, yet I sensed it was my mother braiding Eleanor's hair. The image surged brightly and died out. A brush lay on the table. I stared at the tarnished silver, the match to my mother's hand mirror that Eleanor had smashed against the wall— the brush that had been missing since my mother died. I ran the soft golden bristles over my palm.

The rocking chair began moving, back and forth, back and forth, as if someone were in it. Eleanor had her hands up to her face.

"What is it?" I asked. "Tell me."

"I don't . . . I don't know." She looked stricken, like some memory was trying to come back to her.

A baby cried. The tiny particles shifted and shimmered in the moonlight until I could see the faint shape of a woman reaching toward the cradle. She rubbed the backs of her fingers across the baby's cheek. I touched my own face and felt the tears. The woman lifted the baby and rocked it in her arms, humming softly. I stood there, swaying to the haunting and long-forgotten sound. Then another shape formed beside the rocking chair, a girl, her arms folded across her chest, glaring at the woman with her baby. She glared like Eleanor when she got jealous.

"That's you," I whispered. "And my mother. You're mad at her because she's holding me."

"No, it isn't me," she said, but her voice faltered.

"Yes!" I said, thinking my worst fear was coming true, that Eleanor had hurt my mother after all because she was jealous of me.

The girl's image seemed to throb in anger as she glared at the mother and child. I tried to move in closer, to tell my mother I was right there with her, but she faded away. The girl's image burned a fiery red, her jealousy a throbbing presence in the cave, before it died out.

I stared at Eleanor in horror. I'd been so stupid. Of *course* my mother wanted her to go away. I'd just seen her with my mother, seen her jealousy with my own eyes. I'd been led to the cave so I could see Eleanor's jealousy, so I'd know she had harmed my mother and was a threat to me as well.

"I want to know everything that happened," I

demanded. "Everything!" I moved toward her, feeling such fury at her betrayal that it frightened me but before I could reach her, she turned herself into a gust of wind and blew out of the cave.

"Eleanor! You come back here," I shouted. "What did you do to my mother?"

The light began to dim and I looked up through the stone opening to see a dark shadow crossing the full moon, like the earth was tilting, leaving a crescent sliver behind.

I raced from the cave and scrambled up the side of the cliff, not caring about the rocks below. Sharp thorns bit into my skin, but I smacked them aside, crying, running toward home. A cloud released the moon, but I could tell from the still air that it wasn't *my* crescent moon. This moon was from some other time.

I heard twigs snap up ahead and stumbled to a halt, holding my breath, waiting. Someone was approaching. Then I saw the woman walking the same path I'd seen her on before.

Her white nightgown flickered through the trees like a moon flying through clouds. She stumbled and fell. I tried to run to her, but a fog swirled around my feet, slowing me down. She was coughing and calling out, but I couldn't hear a word she was saying. She struggled to her feet, her hair wild and tangled around her head, and stood there swaying. Then she slowly sank to her knees, fell on her side, and was still.

I moved toward her, drove my legs through that fog, pressed at the dirt so hard it slipped from under my feet like wet sand when the surf pulls back a wave. I could barely breathe when I reached her and fell to my knees.

"Mother?" I whispered.

Her face scarlet with fever, her eyes glazed, she looked toward the cliff and said, "Oh, my dear friend."

My eye caught sudden movement on the path. My father and Aunt Ethel came running in slow motion, as if the air were as thick as honey. My father looked different somehow, younger. But when he spotted my mother on the ground, the pain on his face made him look a hundred years old.

He mouthed her name—"Rose!"—but I couldn't hear it. "Rose," his lips said over and over again.

When he finally reached her, finally fell to the ground and pulled her into his arms, I saw her face clearly for the first time, the face I'd always longed to see, a face that looked so much like my own. When my father's cries caught up to my ears, "Rose!" careened around the clearing, echoed through the trees, and filled me to overflowing.

Her eyes fluttered open and she stared right through me. Then, for one instant, she focused on my eyes. Her gaze hooked into my heart and she tried to speak. I bent down and leaned my face next to hers. She stared at me, and I swear she could really see me, her eyes shining like I was the most beautiful thing she had ever seen. She whispered, "Ivy. Oh Ivy, I'm sorry." Her breath brushed against my face like a moth's wing. It smelled of jasmine. I sucked it in, that breath, drew it right into my body and held it in my lungs. Then I rested my face against her chest and listened to her heart, fluttering like the tiniest bird.

My face passed right through her body when my father lifted her from the ground. He and Aunt Ethel walked toward the house and I started to follow, but I sensed Eleanor waiting below, and I ran to the cliff instead.

I could see the men clearly as I neared the point. A fierce wind blew tails of dirt around their feet and shook the trees they hacked at with sharp machetes. One man, a machete resting on his shoulder, was staring out to sea just like Eleanor always did. He pointed suddenly and everyone rushed to the edge of the cliff.

I watched a ship come into view, a graceful, three-masted schooner, its square and triangle sails pasted to a black sky, as it sailed in the direction of the main harbor at the other end of Mystic Island. An orange light flamed suddenly and blinded me for an instant. More lights flickered. The men were shouting, as they charged around hurriedly to stacks of branches—pyres, which flamed alive, one after another, along the cliff. Then the ship altered course like the other ship had and headed for the burning pyres, and Boneyard Reef in its path.

The men started down the hill on the steep path and disappeared. I crawled closer to the edge of the cliff. A dark school of boats carrying the men slid out of the shadows below and waited silently for the ship like deadly sharks. I crawled out even further until I could see the far end of the beach. And there was Eleanor. But she wasn't staring out to sea, or watching the ship sail closer and closer to the reef. This time she was watching me.

I called to her, all of my anger and uncertainty gone. I called to her with the same love and urgency my mother had just shown, because I finally knew that my mother *had* died of the flu like I'd been told. I had just seen her die exactly like my father and aunt had described. And I knew my mother would never have said, "Oh, my dear friend," if she thought Eleanor was bad or dangerous.

But why did my mother want to send her away? Eleanor still stood on the beach, watching me, dazed. I realized she couldn't give me the answer, because she didn't know. The air grew still and I felt a presence. Was it my mother? Could she tell me?

With my eyes squeezed shut, my fists balled, I focused all of my energy, and I called on my mother for the truth.

Without warning, a force more powerful than any I could have imagined took hold of me, wrenched me right out of my body, and in a raging cyclone of wind and light, whirled me through time and space. I heard Eleanor crying my name, begging me to answer. The energy that controlled us was so powerful even she couldn't resist it. I grabbed hold of Eleanor and held on with every bit of my strength. We spun through the maelstrom, clinging to each other in terror, until the wind died, and we tumbled onto the deck of the ship heading for Boneyard Reef.

All along the cliff the lights flickered like a town lit up at night, and I finally understood why the ship had turned away from its original course, why the first ship I'd seen and so many others must have done the same thing, giving Boneyard Reef its name. They were lured onto the reef by shipwreckers. The lights on the cliff deceived the sailors into thinking they had reached the main port. When the ships crashed on the reef, shipwreckers would steal their cargo.

Unsuspecting sailors crawled high up in the ship's rigging, trimming square sails for the new course. Foamy white spindrift blew from the tops of curling waves.

The captain gripped the wheel, his brows pulled together in concentration. "Didn't think we'd see those lights for several hours yet," he said to a sailor standing beside him. "Current's running swift tonight." He turned the helm over to the other man.

The deck shifted under my feet like when Eleanor had me walk on water, and I squeezed her hand tighter. A woman was standing near the rail staring off at the lights in the distance. A small boy, about four or five years old, sat on the deck next to her. He pulled the hem of her long dress across the top of his head and held it at the back like a bandana. He jabbed a flat piece of wood in the air like a sword. "Mama, I'm a pirate. Look!"

The mother tugged her dress away with one hand. "Behave, Matthew. You should be in your bunk asleep, not making a bother of yourself." I realized she was holding a baby in one arm, wrapped tightly in a warm blanket.

A man approached and the boy stood and ran to him. "We're almost there, Papa." The father smiled and looked away. A girl walked up and handed him a steaming mug. It was Eleanor, but Eleanor in another time. A braid was coiled around her head, neat and elegant, unlike the time I'd done her hair. Her long gray dress brushed the wooden deck.

Silvery tears ran down Eleanor's face as she watched herself. I slipped my arm around her waist and held her tight.

The little boy said, "Papa, are you sure we have a big house? And the slate roof is really red? And we'll get two dogs, not one?"

Eleanor said, "And I get my own room, Father, with the willow tree outside the window."

The baby began to cry. Eleanor turned and watched intently as the woman soothed the infant. I recognized the jealous look in her eyes.

"Mother, will you brush my hair?" Eleanor unpinned her braid and began to unwind it.

"Not now, dear. You see I'm busy."

Eleanor's eyes flashed. "You're *always* busy with the baby. I look a fright." She tossed her hair loose and walked to her mother. "You promised. You haven't brushed it once since we left."

The woman raised the crying infant to her shoulder and didn't respond.

Eleanor stamped her foot. "It's so unfair! You never have time for me!"

Her father looked at her sternly.

Her mother said, "Don't be rude, dear. It doesn't become you."

The father grunted and turned away. He raised the mug toward his mouth, but lowered it without taking a drink. He pushed past Eleanor and moved quickly toward the rail.

He dropped the mug on the deck and stared in disbelief at the white-water waves crashing on the jagged reef. I felt Eleanor stiffen and back away from me, as if she knew what was coming and couldn't bear to watch it.

The man raced to the helm.

"John, what is it?" the woman cried out. He grabbed the wheel away from the sailor on watch and spun it hard to starboard. But too late. The ship climbed onto the reef. It hung there suspended in air like a dragonfly and time stood still. Then it rolled on its side and shuddered. A man fell from the rigging and his head cracked open on the deck like a melon. Other men dangled from ropes above, their faces twisted in terror, while scraps of torn sail scattered in the air like white geese.

The ship heeled violently, and Eleanor and her little brother began to slide down the deck. The ship groaned and heaved, and the mother dropped the baby in her arms. It slipped away like a sack of laundry.

"John, help!"

A boom swung out of control and smashed into her husband, knocking him overboard as he tried to get back to her and his children.

"Matthew!" the woman screamed as her son slid by her feet and disappeared.

Eleanor tried to stand, but a lifeboat swung from its brace and clipped her head. She went down to her knees, her hair wet and scraggly against her bleeding face. Shredded sails snapped at her eyes in the angry wind.

A blanket rolled across the deck, unraveled like a bolt of cloth, and came to rest against the railing, spilling out a naked baby girl. Her tiny fists pummeled the air in terror and pain as her little bald head scraped against harsh ropes. Passengers and crew were screaming, scrambling over one another, looking for safety that didn't exist.

Eleanor clawed her way toward her mother and reached out her hand. "Mother, please help me!"

The mother crawled to Eleanor, then the baby spilled toward her in a wave across the deck. The mother turned away from Eleanor and tried to grab the baby as it floated closer. The ship lifted and smashed against the jagged reef and splintered open.

"Mother! Please!" Eleanor tried to drag herself closer

to her mother. I tried to reach her myself. But I was powerless, trapped in another dimension of time.

She stretched both arms toward her mother, her eyes wide with terror, but hysterical and panicked, the mother reached for the infant instead. It was the last thing Eleanor saw before she washed through a gaping hole in the ship and disappeared into the sea.

Dark shapes were gliding toward the reef, boats carrying the shipwreckers who would kill survivors and scavenge the ship's bounty. The wind whined in the broken rigging. I remembered my own Eleanor then. In my fear, I'd left her alone to watch herself die. I crawled over the deck, searching and calling her name. Something glowed in the water just below the surface. It was a face, shimmery and iridescent—Eleanor's face as I'd first seen it underwater at the reef. It swelled, became bloated and grotesque, and I covered my eyes, pressed the heels of my hands into them to blot out the vision. But when I looked again, the image in the water erupted into a fiery funnel that seemed filled with pain and rage. It was Eleanor's spirit, the angry spirit of a girl who thought her mother had abandoned her for another child. The cyclone raged around and around the broken ship, trailing liquid fire through the air, until it soared away and disappeared.

The shipwreckers were crawling through the smashed rigging, clubs in their hands, moving toward me. Could they see me? Was I going to die on Boneyard Reef like Eleanor? I closed my eyes and visualized myself as a flaming vortex of energy, whirling through time and space. When I opened my eyes, I was alone on the cliff, staring at the empty sea. Eleanor and her ship were gone.

TEN

I searched everywhere, calling her name quietly as I got closer to the house. But I couldn't find her. The beach was deserted, too, when I got there, the last place I could think to look. I sat heavily on the cool sand and dropped my head on my knees. I hugged my legs tightly. There was no place left to search. A wave rolled up and covered my toes in white foam. The crescent moon that had always looked like a lopsided grin when I was a little girl seemed like a menacing leer.

I still didn't understand why my mother wanted to send Eleanor away. Was it because of the jealousy? Had my mother brought me to Eleanor's ship so I could see her rage and know she was a threat to me? A night heron flew by and frightened me.

I jumped up and walked along the edge of the surf toward the dock. Salty water stung the scratches on my ankles.

"Eleanor," I called softly.

Waves slapped under the boards of the dock, squirting small jets of water through the cracks. I was wondering if she could be in the cave when the air filled with jasmine. I pressed my foot on the bow of the skiff and stepped aboard. My palms grew sweaty as I looked across the dark water toward the other end of the island. Then I started the engine and steered toward town.

I almost missed the small cove where I always anchored for school, the coastline barely visible against the night. I tread gingerly on the sand, afraid of crunching down on the millions of crabs I imagined were scuttling around my bare feet.

Twice I lost my way on darkened streets. A streetlamp glinted on a red slate roof. I approached and stood in front of the house where I'd first smelled the jasmine so long ago. The house looked hollow, the windows bare of curtains. The white gate creaked like dried bones as I passed through. Once again, the door eased open on its own.

The house seemed to throb, a steady rhythm like the blood pumping through my heart.

"Eleanor," I whispered. Her name echoed like it had in the cave.

I found her standing in a room near the back of the house, arms folded across her chest. Wet, shiny eyes betrayed the pain she was trying to hide.

I placed my hand on her wrist. "Eleanor, all of that happened long ago. You're safe now." She sniffed, but wouldn't admit her sadness.

"You have to tell me, Eleanor. Why did my mother want to send you away? Do you remember now?"

She looked hurt and shook her head. "I only know that she's the one who summoned me in the first place. Just like you did. I was her friend."

Her response knocked the breath out of me. "What

are you talking about? *We* summoned you? Don't be ridiculous. You haunted us on your own."

"I most certainly did not!"

"You did too! No one *summons* a ghost! You just haunt people. That's what ghosts do."

She shook her head in annoyance. "Rose lived alone in your house, just like you. And she was lonely, too, just like you. She summoned me to be her friend." Eleanor turned and walked to the window. "Rose was my friend," she murmured. "We played in the cave and no one else ever came there. Until that baby."

"What? How many years were you together?" I had assumed Eleanor had only come when my mother got older. Now I realized they were the two girls I'd seen in the cave.

Eleanor evaded my eyes, trying to hide her confusion, not understanding my questions about time. "She summoned me," she repeated. "Just like you."

I didn't believe for a minute that we'd summoned her, but I knew my mother had grown up in that house and that she'd remained there with my father after they married.

"Well, I don't know what my mother did." My voice was shaky. "But I never summoned you, that's for sure." Eleanor's eyes softened when she saw I was getting upset.

"Yes, you did, Ivy. You brought me into the water with you near that horrid reef. At first I thought you were Rose."

"Oh," I gasped, pressing my hand on my mouth. I had been feeling the worst loneliness ever that day and wishing I could have a friend. But I certainly didn't have the power to conjure ghosts. Or did I?

"Rose was my friend," she said wistfully. "Then everything changed. That man came. And the baby." She turned back to me. "She wanted to send me away because of that baby."

"The man is my father, Eleanor. And that baby was me. Rose is my mother."

Her brows pulled together in concentration. I saw she couldn't understand that my mother had grown up, that I had been the baby and grown up, too.

"She must have thought you would hurt me," I said. "That's why she wanted to send you away." I wasn't prepared for her shocked and angry reaction.

"I would never have hurt Rose like that. Never! I loved her. But then she went away. I wouldn't help her, so she went away. She didn't love me."

"Eleanor, she died. On the path, when she was trying to reach you. She was sick and died."

She pushed her chin out, because she couldn't understand.

"People die, Eleanor. Like the people on the ship, remember? You died." I spoke softly, not wanting to upset her.

Her eyes cleared in thought, but then they darkened again. "That woman on the ship didn't love me, either. She let me die. She sent me away like Rose wanted to."

I could feel the most awful pain behind the look on her face. "That was your mother, Eleanor. Of *course* she loved you."

Eleanor's eyes filled with tears.

"She was in a panic," I said. "She just reached out to the baby. She couldn't help herself."

"She could have reached out to me."

My heart was breaking for her. "Your mother loved you, Eleanor. And Rose loved you, too. She called you her dear friend. I heard her. She couldn't help leaving you. She was trying to reach you on the beach when she died."

"Rose loved me?" When the tears ran down her face, the scent of jasmine filled the room.

"Eleanor, you have to try to remember. If you weren't going to hurt me, why did my mother want to send you away?"

"I don't know. She saw something when she was standing by this house, something that had to do with you. She said I couldn't die on the reef. I had to live." Eleanor walked back to the window. "But she didn't have enough power to keep my ship off the reef herself. I had to *want* to live or she couldn't do it. Only I didn't want to leave her, so I wouldn't help. And then she went away."

My mind was reeling. "How could my mother keep your ship off the reef, even with your help?"

"I don't know," Eleanor said. "With that same power you have, I guess."

"Me?" I cried, shocked.

"Yes, like when you bring the man back before he wants to come."

"What are you talking about? What man?"

"The man who follows the fish."

"My father? I never brought my father back."

"You did so. I saw you do it when you first summoned me." She stepped closer and looked into my eyes. "You turned those fish around and made his boat follow them so he would come home. But when you saw me, you let him go."

I stared at her in disbelief. But I remembered all the times I'd envisioned schools of fish moving toward the island, so my father would follow them for a good catch and come home sooner than he'd planned. I thought I only pretended, but I must have been using some power I didn't know I had. And even when I didn't use my power to bring him home, I always knew in advance exactly when he'd return. The only thing I couldn't do was keep him home.

Eleanor was gazing out the window watching the weeping willow, its trailing branches dancing on the ground.

"Rose loved me," she murmured.

"Yes, she did," I said. "Eleanor, I have to get home, it's getting light. Come with me."

She didn't move. "My ship is coming, Ivy."

My chest tightened. "Well, there's nothing we can do about that. Come with me. I have to get back before my aunt wakes up."

She said, "Rose needed me to help her keep the ship off the reef, but I refused. I can do what she wanted now, Ivy, if you'll help."

Her words made me light-headed as I realized what she was asking. "Well, you better forget it. Come on, I'll take you for a ride in my boat instead."

"Ivy—"

"Forget it," I said. "Don't even *think* about it. You're a ghost and that's that."

"I need your help, Ivy."

"No! I don't have any of that power you said. Besides,

if I help you stay alive, you won't be a ghost anymore. You're *my* friend now. You can't leave. I won't let you go."

"My ship is coming, Ivy. Rose brought it back once before. She said it took all of her power to do it. She may never be able to bring it back again. I have to leave now. Rose would never have wanted to send me away unless it was important. She loved me. She must want you to help. That's why the ship's coming back again. Please, Ivy."

I was stunned. My mother was bringing Eleanor's ship back to take her away? How could she *do* that to me?

"I don't care about your stupid ship. What are you doing haunting people in the first place? Haunting my mother—haunting me—and then you just leave when you feel like it? What do you expect me to do, anyway? How am I supposed to keep your ship from crashing on the reef?"

I stormed outside. "If I help you, will you still be a ghost?" The words caught in my throat. "Will you stay here with me?"

She didn't answer. She didn't have to. I knew the answer already.

"*No!*" I shouted. "I won't help you. I won't!" I rushed outside and Eleanor followed. I felt a touch on my hand and knew it was my mother. All along it was my mother who'd been haunting me, causing the visions, moving me through time. Why? So she could take my only friend away?

"Ivy, wait!" Eleanor appeared in front of me.

"Why did you haunt my mother in the first place? She died because of you. Dropped dead right there on that stupid path, trying to help you. And there was nothing she could have done. Just like there's nothing I can do."

"You have the power, Ivy."

I turned away so Eleanor couldn't see my lips tremble. The scab on my hand throbbed, the crescent scab that looked like the moon overhead.

I made my hand into a fist. "I don't care!" I punched at the air, drove my fist toward the sky. "I won't help you. I hate you. I hate you both!"

I raced back to the boat and sped home. Aunt Ethel was banging on my door as I climbed through the window. Tripping over the sill, I crashed to the floor and kicked a chair across the room as hard as I could.

"What's going on in here?" She opened the door and her mouth fell open.

"Oh, my heavens! Look at you! What have you been up to? For pity's sake." She moved toward me. "You'll be the death of me yet."

"*Good!*" I was breathless with anger. "I hope I *am* the death of you. I *want* to be the death of you!"

My aunt stumbled back in shock. Never once had I raised my voice to her. I slammed the door in her face and changed quickly into clean clothes.

Eleanor was watching me from outside the window. I grabbed at the shade and yanked it all the way down, but it snapped back up, furled like the world chart in front of Mr. Gerber's skeleton. I smacked the shells onto the floor, snatched up the long white feather and smashed it onto the sill until the fragile quill was snapped and bent from top to bottom. I tossed it out the window at Eleanor.

I finished dressing and ran out the door without breakfast, without saying good-bye to my aunt. My first class had already started when I got there, and I stomped on Sharon's foot as I passed her desk.

She leaped out of her seat. "Miss Lowell, Ivy stepped on my foot!"

I turned and said, "It was an accident, Miss Lowell."

"Well, she should apologize, anyway," Sharon whined.

"I'm sorry, Sharon. I didn't realize your feet were so big."

One of Sharon's girlfriends snorted and Sharon gave her a look that squashed her like a bug.

Miss Lowell said, "Girls! That's enough."

I walked down the rest of the aisle and knocked into every knee I could. As I went to sit down, the skeleton bones began to clack.

Eleanor was hanging inside it, *wearing* it, like the skeleton's bones were her very own. She was very faint and misty like it was taking all of her strength to make herself visible. Or maybe she just had no strength left because her ship was so near.

She tried to lift the skeleton's arm, make it scratch itself like she'd done in the past to make me laugh. But the bones fell back down and dangled lifelessly. Sharon bustled over to shut the window when Miss Lowell said it must be a draft stirring the skeleton. Rain sprinkled the pane and I thought Eleanor was going to soak Sharon like she'd done the last time she'd wanted to make up with me. But the window didn't open after Sharon closed it, and only a few drops of rain slid down the glass like tears.

She hung around me all day—lifting ponytails, scattering homework and tests, squeaking chalk on the blackboard. I wouldn't acknowledge her. Not even a smile. Not once. I knew what she was trying to do. She was trying to please me, trying to make me care about her so much that I'd want to do what she asked. But I wouldn't. No matter what she did, I wouldn't let her go.

I thought she'd be waiting at the skiff when classes ended, but she wasn't there. When I climbed into the boat, I found a gold coin on the seat. It was worn and dull, not like the first one Eleanor had given me, the brilliant gold coin I'd thrown at her and never found again. I stuffed it in my pocket but kept my eyes down as I raised the anchor.

The wind was picking up after all, the waves getting larger, and spindrift blew from the tops like snapping rags. I was halfway home when the bird descended from the sky. It was a crane, like the other two cranes we'd seen when we first met, only smaller this time. It landed right in the bow of the boat and sort of staggered toward me. One wing was lower than the other and dragged as it tried to walk. When it lifted its head to trumpet, only a cracked squawk came out, and one of its eyes was stuck shut. It moved closer and raised a crooked wing toward my face. Gently, so gently, it brushed my cheek like a feathery kiss.

"I hate you," I whispered.

It spread its wings, the feathers droopy and ragged, the velvet black tips now faded and grayish. It tried to take off, but its foot, yellow and cracked like a dead chicken's, clipped the edge of the bow. The bird spilled into the water and lifted its large wing up and down against the surface, trying to stay afloat. A feather floated toward the boat, but I refused to reach for it.

"I won't help you, Eleanor."

The bird sank out of sight.

The wind was strengthening, the sky darkening, and a wave slapped over the bow and drenched my bookbag. Eleanor didn't try any more tricks to win me over, and I expected to see her standing on the beach staring at the horizon. But she wasn't there. The skiff started to roll dangerously and I tried to steer it closer to the wind so it wouldn't capsize. I throttled the engine higher to make headway, but the boat barely moved against the wind. More water broke over the side and I started to bail.

When I looked up, I felt the blood drain from my face. A line squall was heading right toward me, a black wall of wind and rain. I watched it move closer and closer. It hit me with the force of a blow and turned the day to night as if the moon had passed in front of the sun.

As quickly as the squall had struck, everything got still and silent—and Eleanor's ship sailed out of the dark.

ELEVEN

I throttled the motor as high as I could and wheeled my skiff in another direction. The air around me was black and thick. I couldn't see a thing, but I kept steering away from Eleanor's ship. Finally, I motored out of the blackness, like coming out of a tunnel at night, and I thought I was back in my own world again.

It was too dark to see the dock ahead, but the island was visible and I turned the boat toward shore. As I got in close, the hair rose on the back of my neck. Four empty boats near the shore were tugging on their anchors in the wind. I looked over my shoulder, but Eleanor's ship was no longer in sight, and when I stared up at the ridge of the cliff it was empty.

Then a man—the man I'd seen before—stepped into view and leaned against a tree, a machete resting on his shoulder. I fell back in fright and the tiller slipped out of my hand. The boat lurched and headed straight for one of the small boats. Before I could grab the tiller again, my bow reached the other boat. My skiff passed through it like a knife through air.

I was relieved that I couldn't feel or move anything

from the past. There was nothing I could do to help Eleanor even if I wanted to. I anchored the boat near shore and thought of running along the beach to go home the other way, but I looked back up at the man standing there waiting for Eleanor's ship and I started to climb up the steep path.

When I got to the top, I cried out in shock and lost my footing. I had put my hands on the man's shoes, right through them. I was shaking all over as I moved to the side and climbed back up. I knew he couldn't see me and hadn't felt my hands on his feet, but I didn't care. He looked so real.

I stood at the edge of the cliff. Men chopped at the trees with their machetes. They were dressed poorly, trouser cuffs torn or frayed at the ends, and one had no shoes. Another man was missing an eye. He didn't even have a patch over the puckered hole. One of them shook a bottle over the piles of branches and I figured it must be something to make the wood burn.

A big man with a dark shadow of a beard scowled and charged me and I stumbled backward and fell. He marched right through me and I cried out. No one heard me. He snatched the bottle away from the man who was pouring, drank the remains, and then flung it over the cliff.

My knees were shaking when I got back up. Eleanor's ship still wasn't in sight and I remembered my mother. Was she on her way to help Eleanor stay alive? Or was she already lying on the ground, dying for her efforts? I ran across the clearing to go to her.

A sudden shout spun me around and the man keeping

watch pointed with his machete. The other men sprang into action. Someone grabbed a club with something black and sticky like tar at the end and struck a match to light it. The man on watch raised his hand to stop him and said gruffly, "Not yet! When it's closer."

I watched Eleanor's ship in the distance, sailing a safe course for the main harbor at the other end of Mystic Island. I pictured her on the ship, a beautiful girl my age. My heart ached with the knowledge that there was no way I could help her even if I wanted to.

So many memories flooded my mind. I saw her standing in my backyard wearing my dress that first time. I saw her leaping around like crazy, trumpeting with those cranes. I saw her soaking Sharon and being the only friend I had at school. I remembered every day, every gift, every nice thing she'd done—and every mean trick too, which didn't make me love her one bit less.

A loud voice barked, "*Light the fires!*" The torch flamed alive.

I raced to the edge of the cliff. Eleanor's ship was still sailing a safe course. I realized I could *never* let her suffer—no matter how much I wanted her to stay. I looked around wildly, wondering what I could do. I ran to one of the unlit pyres and tried to pull a branch away. But my hand passed right through it. Again and again I tried. I even pushed at the torch being used to light the fire, but my arm fanned right through the air.

I stared at the ship and let my love for Eleanor fill me up. I willed my love to keep her ship on its safe course. I drew on every bit of power I had. But the ship came around slowly, turned right in towards land like it had before, and started sailing toward the reef. I didn't give up, didn't stop feeling that love, not for a second. I charged the air with it, so Eleanor might somehow live, even though it meant losing her forever.

Her ship started to radiate light. Like melting silver, an iridescent glow ran over the deck, slowly along the ropes, through the rigging, from the bottom of the mast to the top. Every sail lit up like a sheet of silver on a velvet cloth.

Someone shouted behind me and I turned quickly. Men were pointing at the ship, their eyes wide with fear. A voice cried out, "A ghost ship!" Not all of the fires were lit, but the man with the torch dropped it and started to back away. Others bumped into each other, scrambling to run away. Only the man on watch stood there, calling them back, but no one listened.

Eleanor's ship was still heading toward the reef, still fixed on the burning fires on the cliff. I couldn't put them out. There was no way I could put them out. The man was staring right through me, angry that the others had left. I stared at him, glared right into his eyes, and willed myself to appear. Slowly at first, like a spark tended by the wind, my body started to glow. It flamed brighter and brighter. The man cried out and stumbled backward.

"What *are* you?" he shouted. He moved toward me, his face contorted in fear. He swung the machete at me and I sparkled like luminescent water. "Get away from here!"

He kept coming and I backed toward the fires, uncertain about what I intended to do.

He lunged at me with the blade and I jumped back, right off the cliff and into the air. I started to drop. Sharp broken branches tore at my face and arms as I tried to stop my fall. I grabbed onto a thick vine and my arm wrenched in the socket, but I held on, my face pressed against the sour earth, trying to find a foothold.

Burning pieces of trees and leaves suddenly rained down around me. I looked up. The man was kicking the fires at me from the cliff. I hung there in a shower of falling embers. As soon as the lights on the cliff disappeared, Eleanor's silver ship turned away from the reef, its sails billowing with fresh wind.

Watching her ship sail away, knowing I would never see Eleanor again, I grew weak and my fingers loosened on the vine. But a powerful force gripped my hand and I knew it was my mother. Although she had sent the ship to take Eleanor away, I trusted her love. I drew strength from her love—and I closed my fist on the vine and hung on.

Cautiously, my foot wedged in a shallow depression in the face of the cliff, I began my slow descent. But a rock broke away and threw me off balance. I lost my footing and rolled all the way to the bottom and hit my head. The same burning stars that had spilled from the cliff exploded before my eyes. I started to spin, to whirl through space, and disappeared into a silent abyss.

TWELVE

I hear soft voices and feel someone holding my hand. I smell alcohol and remember the doctor's office when I was little and about to get an injection. I'm glad to drift away again before I dream about someone sticking a needle in me.

I open my eyes and I see a tube running from the sky down to my body. A woman in white is standing over me. An angel, I think. A voice in a tunnel says, "Wake up, Ivy. Wake up."

The angel, I notice, is wearing a name tag. The letters swim around like tadpoles and I close my eyes.

"Wake up, Ivy. Everything's all right." The angel takes my hand. "We're taking good care of you. You're safe now."

My voice is slurred. "Am I in heaven?"

The angel smiles. "No, Ivy. You're in the hospital. You had a nasty fall, but you'll be fine. Are you thirsty?" She turns to another woman in white. "She can suck on ice chips. Nothing more today."

Aunt Ethel appears. She stands by my bed, her hands clasped tightly together in front of her stomach. I remember shouting at her.

The angel is holding my wrist. She frowns and looks down at me. "It's all right, Ivy. You don't have to be afraid now. You're safe."

I reach out to my aunt and she grabs my fingers. Her lips are pressed together tightly. I drift in and out of sleep feeling lonely, but I can't remember why. Whenever I open my eyes, my aunt is always there, and sometimes the angel.

Aunt Ethel cranked my bed to help raise me up. "Now, don't you worry about a thing. Everything's going to be fine. Eat. Eat. For pity's sake, that's all they give you for days? Why would anyone think green Jell-O is good for a person? Not even a banana in it. It's a wonder you don't starve to death right here in the hospital. Wouldn't that be lovely?"

"Dr. Barrett said I can eat solid food tomorrow, Aunt Ethel. She said I'd puke my guts out if I ate before then." I tapped my spoon on top of the green Jell-O to make it wobble.

"Well, I'm sure those weren't her words." She plumped my pillow carefully and fussed at the white sheet and almost spilled my tray. She kept tugging at the sheet, folding it over a thin blanket at my waist, talking away to herself like I wasn't even there. "Lucky to be alive. A young girl like that, having to beach a boat in a storm and falling off a cliff on the way home from school." She gave the sheet a hard yank to tuck it in.

"You're cutting off the circulation in my legs, Aunt Ethel."

She puffed out a big breath of air. "Well, now, I just wanted to get you settled. Visiting hours are almost over. Like a prison here." She smoothed the sheet gently beside the hand with the IV needle in the skin. Her lips were drawn together in a tight white line.

"I'm okay, Aunt Ethel, honest. Don't worry. Dr. Barrett said I'll be off the IV tomorrow and can have real food. And the operation went fine. You can go back to the motel now. You don't have to spend so much time here. I'll see you in the morning."

As she turned to walk away, I said, "Aunt Ethel, did you find a coin in my pocket? When you took my clothes away, was there a coin or anything?"

"A coin? No. Like what, a quarter? No, only dirt and burrs and goodness knows what. Do you want some change? Here, I'll leave my change purse. For what, a soda? Don't pay for a thing. It'll show up on the bill, anyway. But keep the change. Here, I'll put it right by the phone."

"That's okay. I was just wondering." I closed my eyes and took a deep breath.

"Now you just press that little button there if you want anything. Anything at all. That's what it's for. If your head hurts, just push the button down and hold it." She snatched it up and pressed her thumb on it. She'd done the same thing the day before. Then she stood there waiting to see how long it would take for the nurse to come in. "A person could be dead by the time they get here."

"Call me from the motel to say good night, Aunt Ethel, okay?"

The nurse came in and my aunt made a big production of looking at her watch.

"Sorry," I said. "I accidentally leaned on the button."

Aunt Ethel marched out with her shoulders arched.

When the nurse took my tray away, I made her leave the rolling table across my lap. I lifted the top and stared at myself in the small mirror. One of my eyes had a dark smudge under it, and the cheek below was red and swollen. It looked like a small bird had run all over the rest of my face leaving tiny red tracks. I ran my fingers down the white bandage that covered my entire head. Every bit of my hair was gone. Dr. Barrett said they had to shave it to operate and remove the pressure on my brain. But she promised it would all grow back.

The Coast Guard had finally located my father and he'd be there by the next day. They still hadn't found my boat and figured it broke up in the squall and washed away. I hoped it was never found. But at least I wouldn't have to go back to school, even if they did find it.

Aunt Ethel would *never* let me go to school in a boat again. She'd made that very clear.

My father got there early the next morning and the nurses let him in even though visiting hours hadn't begun. My throat tightened when I saw his face. It looked just like it had when he'd found my mother on the path. He stood there not knowing what to do, staring at the needle in my hand, the tube sliding up to the IV bag. He was afraid to touch me, afraid he'd hurt me somehow.

"Hello, Daddy."

He cleared his throat, trying to speak, but he couldn't at first.

"The squall came up real sudden, Daddy, so I figured it was best to turn in and get off the water. But everything's okay now. My head will be as good as new." His hands were in tight fists at his sides and the knuckles had bled white. He only stayed for a little while because my eyes were getting droopy.

His voice was hoarse. "I'll be back later, Ivy. You sleep now."

I had tried not to think about Eleanor, tried not to picture her face or her ship sailing away. I couldn't wait to go home. That's all I wanted to do. Go home and start homeschooling again with my aunt. Things would never be the same again, I knew that. But at least I'd be finished with school and with that mean Sharon, finished with feeling like I didn't belong. I could swim the reef, and shell on the beach, and maybe someday I would stop missing Eleanor and start feeling happy again. I was surprised to feel tears running down my cheeks.

I felt much better by the time my father and aunt returned late that afternoon. Dad was still pale, but smiling.

"We have good news for you, Ivy," my aunt said. "Tell her, Albert."

My father said, "Your aunt and I went to a real-estate agent. We found a nice house right here in town. It's empty and we'll be moved in before you even get out of the hospital. No more being all alone at the end of the island. You can walk to school now with all the other kids." He rested his hand on top of mine. "Everything's going to be fine now, Ivy. Just fine."

When he finished speaking, I closed my eyes, and I suppose they thought I was so happy I couldn't help but cry.

I stood inside the curtain watching kids pass the house. The filmy material made them look like they were floating by in a mist. The bandage still covered my head and I reached up to make sure my new cap was still in place. I'd been putting off leaving, dreading my first day back to school.

Aunt Ethel slipped my new backpack over my shoulders. "Now, don't you worry. There isn't a girl in that school as pretty as you, even without any hair. And it's growing under there right now, you mark my words. When the bandage comes off next week, you'll already have hair and look like one of those fancy models in your magazines." She edged me toward the door.

I stood on the welcome mat outside and rocked back and forth on the brushy tan pile. Some older kids were passing and I wanted to wait till they were gone. I got to the end of our walk and stepped through the gate.

A voice said, "There you are. I've been waiting forever." A blond girl stood there, her arms folded across her chest. I drew in a breath, thinking at first it was Eleanor.

I tugged my cap down a little further.

"Well, almost forever," she said. "I hate being late for school. Everyone stares at you when you walk in."

She looked at my head. "I like your hat."

I shrugged, but didn't say anything. Then I saw Sharon crossing toward us with one of her friends. "Oh, great," I said under my breath.

"Don't worry. Miss Lowell told everyone they had to be very nice to you because of your injury. You might need one of those airplane bags, though, in case they make you barf."

"Ivy, we're *so* glad you're back," Sharon said, eyeing my cap. Does your head hurt? Aren't you afraid you'll bump it? Maybe you should wear one of those football helmets."

"Maybe *you* should wear one," the blond girl said, "in case *your* head gets bumped."

Sharon said, "Are they sure your hair will grow back? I heard sometimes it doesn't."

The girl got very stern and said, "Be careful! Don't say anything that might upset her. My mother said she has a huge blood blister on her brain and if she gets upset it could explode and splatter brain guts all over the inside of her head."

Sharon looked hesitant, like she wasn't sure whether to believe the girl or not.

The girl said, "You could get the *chair* for killing someone, you know."

Sharon sighed and rolled her eyes. "See you at school, Ivy. If you start failing anything, I'll be happy to help you."

Sharon's friend gave me a little wave as they walked away. "I hate that Sharon," the girl said. "She made fun of my braces my first day at school."

"Brain guts?" I said.

Her eyes were expressionless. "I was only kidding about the blood blister. Actually, my mother made her assistant Igor get you a new brain. But Mom is worried he might have gotten one from a deranged relative of Sharon's."

Then she smiled. Little stars as blue as her eyes lined the rubber band on her braces.

"Who's your mother?" I asked.

"She operated on you. I'm Katie Barrett. Lucky thing for you we just moved here. You were Mom's very first patient at the new hospital. We better go. We're going to be late. Do you want to come over after school?"

I nodded, but acted like I didn't really care.

"I'll stick close to you and make sure nobody bumps your head."

She watched over me all day. When classes ended, she

was waiting. "I have to tell my aunt I'm going to your house," I said.

"Okay. Let's ask if we can do our homework together so you won't have to leave too early."

Aunt Ethel was waiting at the door and I wondered if she'd been standing there all day. "Well, well. Your first day back. Bring your playmate in," she called.

I groaned and was relieved that Katie didn't make any cracks. "This is Katie Barrett," I said. "Is it okay if I go over her house for a while?"

"Barrett? Are you the doctor's girl?"

"Uh-huh. My mother operated on Ivy."

"And she did a very nice job of it. Now, where is your house? I don't want you wandering all over town, Ivy."

"It's down the block. The one with the red slate roof," Katie answered.

"Well, for pity's sake!" Aunt Ethel looked at me. "Why, that's the house your father was trying to buy for your mother before she got sick, bless her soul. Well, well, so that's where you live."

I felt like I was sleepwalking on the way to Katie's. When we got there, it was the jasmine house, just as I knew it would be, looking as friendly and inviting as the first time I saw it.

"We used to live on the mainland," Katie said as we walked in, "but it was so busy and crowded there. When the new hospital was finished, Mom got a job and we came here. I wanted to come over all week and visit you, but I was getting over a cold and my mother didn't want you to catch it. Let's have a snack. Mom always leaves me something."

We sat in the kitchen and ate brownies and drank cold milk. "Is your father a doctor, too?" I asked.

"No, he died when I was little."

"Oh. My father's a fisherman."

"I know, I met him," she said. "He came over with some fish for us because he said my mother saved your life. Swordfish, it was great. We love fish and he said he'd bring us more and Mom said we'd all have a barbecue together."

"My father's going to start a fishing business in town. Take tourists out fishing for the day, so he doesn't have to be away so much."

"Maybe I could go fishing with you someday."

"Maybe," I answered.

We sat there chewing and staring at each other. "This house is haunted, you know. Lots of people have heard a girl crying. My mother thinks it's only the wind, but I know it's a real ghost."

She ran her tongue across a white milk mustache. Her eyes were bright with excitement. "Can you keep a secret?" she asked.

"Yes," I whispered.

"I think there are *two* ghosts."

"Two ghosts?"

She slid her chair in closer and lowered her voice. "The other night I woke up and saw a girl standing by my window. Then another girl walked up behind her."

I barely breathed as she went on. "They were shimmery and I wanted to get close enough to see their faces, but all of a sudden the room smelled of flowers and it made me sleepy. That's all I remember."

Icy shivers ran through me when I pictured myself a ghost like Eleanor. I pinched my arm under the table to be sure I was real again.

"You believe me, don't you?" Katie asked.

She smiled when I nodded.

"Come on, I'll show you my room."

My throat ached as we walked down the narrow hall. Katie didn't notice that I led the way. As we entered her room, I stopped perfectly still and stared at an oil painting on the wall.

"My mother painted that," she said. "She's an artist. I like to draw, too."

I could hardly breathe. "Why did your mother paint this ship?"

"It's supposed to be the one my great-great-grandparents were on. Maybe there was another 'great.' I'm not sure. The whole family sailed here. One of the children was a girl my age, too. It says so in a ship's log we have. This house has always been in my family."

"What was the girl's name?" I whispered.

"Her name? I don't remember. Agatha or Agnes or something like that."

"Oh." I leaned in to read the name painted along the bow. *Eleanor Moneypenny*, it said. The name of the ship was *Eleanor Moneypenny*.

It was hard to speak. "Why is the ship shining? Why is it glowing like that?"

"It's St. Elmo's fire, the way it shines. Did you ever hear of it? It happens to ships sometimes. Something in the atmosphere, maybe when there's a storm. I'm not sure. But the ship, it just lights up. It was kind of eerie. It says in the log that the whole ship just started to glow, then all of a sudden the lights they thought were from the town began to fall from the sky like in a firestorm. And the captain or someone realized they were heading straight for a reef. They would have crashed right into it if those lights hadn't gone out. Good thing for us they realized in time!" She smiled then, and her blue eyes sparkled. "Me and Mom wouldn't have been born if our ancestors had been killed!"

I ran my fingers along the glowing lines of the ship, so shiny and iridescent, like on the night it sailed away. Poor Eleanor hadn't remembered her own name. When I pressed her, she took the only name she could think of, the name of the ship she'd been on. But I didn't care what her real name was. *Eleanor*, that's who she'd always be to me.

The phone rang and Katie ran to answer it. "Mom, is it okay if my friend stays for dinner?"

My friend. Katie had called me her friend. I was stunned by a moment of clarity as dazzling as a full moon. I knew what my mother's vision had been! She'd seen me growing up at the end of Mystic Island, just as she had, alone and without friends. I had always dreamed of moving to town and going to school with other kids. Then Eleanor came and she was all that mattered. The vision must have shown me living in seclusion with her for the rest of my life.

But my mother wanted so much more for me. If I spent my life haunted by the past, I would end up as lonely and unhappy as my father. My mother wanted me to live life among the living.

I heard Katie hang up the phone and gazed at the ship in wonder. Had my mother known that if Eleanor didn't die on the reef, one of her descendants would live in this very house—a girl my own age? I pressed my palm against a sail on the smooth canvas and for the briefest moment I felt my mother's touch. *Oh, yes. She had known.*

Katie ran back into the alcove. "Mom'll be home soon. She said you can stay for dinner, but we have to go ask your aunt."

We walked outside and as we passed in front of her house, she ran her fingers through the tiny white flowers growing along the fence and the air filled with the sweet scent of jasmine. She didn't say a word to me, not one word, as I whispered goodbye to Eleanor, and I bet there wasn't another girl in the whole world who could have let me cry like that without asking one question.

When she slipped her arm through mine, I pressed it against my side—just a little—to hold it tighter. We walked home that way, the two of us, our arms linked together.